Farewell to Earth

DON'T MISS THE REST OF THE
SIXTH-GRADE ALIEN SERIES!

Farewell to Earth

By **BRUCE COVILLE**

Illustrated by Glen Mullaly

ALADDIN

NEW YORK   LONDON   TORONTO   SYDNEY   NEW DELHI

ALADDIN

An imprint of Simon & Schuster Children's Publishing Division

1230 Avenue of the Americas, New York, New York 10020

This Aladdin hardcover edition January 2022

Text copyright © 2001, 2022 by Bruce Coville

Illustrations copyright © 2022 by Glen Mullaly

Also available in an Aladdin paperback edition.

All rights reserved, including the right of reproduction in whole or in part in any form.

ALADDIN and related logo are registered trademarks of Simon & Schuster, Inc.

For information about special discounts for bulk purchases, please contact Simon & Schuster Special Sales at 1-866-506-1949 or business@simonandschuster.com.

The Simon & Schuster Speakers Bureau can bring authors to your live event. For more information or to book an event contact the Simon & Schuster Speakers Bureau at 1-866-248-3049 or visit our website at www.simonspeakers.com.

Designed by Tiara Iandiorio

The illustrations for this book were rendered in a mix of traditional and digital media.

The text of this book was set in Noyh Book.

Manufactured in the United States of America 1221 FFG

2 4 6 8 10 9 7 5 3 1

Library of Congress Control Number 2021946715

ISBN 9781534487406 (hc)

ISBN 9781534487390 (pbk)

ISBN 9781534487413 (ebook)

TO THE GANG AT MFL,
WHO CHEERED ME ON
ALONG THE WAY.

CONTENTS

CHAPTER 1

[PLESKIT]
A LETTER HOME

FROM: Pleskit Meenom, on the soon-to-be-distant Planet Earth
TO: Maktel Geebrit, on my beloved home planet, Hevi-Hevi

Dear Maktel:

This will be the last letter I send you from Earth. Things here have taken a shocking turn, and I wanted to let you know about them as soon as possible.

Actually, I am certain you have already heard something about the recent events, whether on the Interplanetary News or from your Motherly One. But I wanted to give you the inside story. It seemed only fair, since you're going to have to deal with the results yourself before long!

I hope you won't be too upset.

Fremmix Bleeblom!

Your pal,

Pleskit

CHAPTER 2

[PLESKIT]
A BITTER END

When Chris Mellblom walked right past me in the lunchroom without even saying hello, I knew something was wrong. From the very beginning of my stay on Earth, Chris had been one of the kids most willing to be friendly with a purple alien from the planet Hevi-Hevi.

Most willing of all, of course, had been my good friend Tim Tompkins. He and Rafaella Martinez were sitting next to me when Chris walked past.

"What was *that* all about?" asked Rafaella, looking surprised. "Chris is usually a lot nicer than that."

"I do not know," I said, emitting the quiet fart of

3

minor sorrow. Its odor is subtle, and Tim and Rafaella did not even notice it.

"Maybe he's got end-of-the-year jitters," said Tim, ducking a paper airplane thrown at him by Jordan Lynch. "After all, we've got some major tests coming up."

This sentence would turn out to be more true than Tim realized—though the tests we were about to face were not the ones that could have been expected.

"If it was only Chris acting strange, I might agree," I said, shouting to be heard above the cafeteria hubbub. "But he is the third kid to snub me like that today." I sighed. "I am aware that all things must come to an end, but I was hoping sixth grade would have a better ending than this."

"Well, you couldn't ask for better weather!" said Rafaella, trying to be cheerful.

In this regard she was right. Earthlings divide their year into units loosely related to the action of their single, rather small moon. We were currently in the unit called "June," and the sunshine and cool breezes were most pleasant. In less than two weeks the school year would be over.

Personally, I took small comfort in the lovely weather and the approaching vacation—especially when the

Farewell to Earth

next day even more kids began avoiding me or acting uncomfortable in my presence.

"This is definitely weird," said Tim when we went outside for what our teacher, Ms. Weintraub, calls "the Daily Run-Around." (She calls it this because she says we are too old for "playtime." I am glad she does not think we are also too old to need the free time the run-around offers us.) "I tried asking Chris what was up, but he wouldn't say."

"Neither would Michael or Misty," said Rafaella, referring to two other classmates who had refused to talk to me that day.

"You don't suppose this is about Doris, do you?" asked Tim.

Doris used to be one of our class hamsters, until she mutated (for reasons that were only partly my fault) into an intelligent but evil hamsteroid. "Five inches tall and as dangerous as a rattlesnake," is how my bodyguard, Robert McNally, liked to describe her. The reason Doris was still on everyone's minds was that, as far as we knew, she was living inside the walls of the school, which made us all a bit nervous.

The school authorities had tried to catch her, of

5

course, but setting traps for Doris was a little tricky, since she tended to do something even worse in response. The last trap they had put out for her had ended up on the chair of our principal, Mr. Grand, causing a very painful accident to his bottom parts.

As I've said, Doris was not merely intelligent, she was dangerous.

Even so, I didn't think she could be the root of the current problem.

Neither did Tim. "I don't see why the kids would be any more upset about Doris now than they were last week, or the week before," he said.

Rafaella shrugged. "Sometimes these things build up in people's minds."

As it turned out, whatever was building up, it wasn't just in the minds of my classmates.

When I left school that day, I saw something I hadn't seen since the early days of my visit to this planet: a group of protesters waving signs with angry slogans such as "Alien, Go Home!" and "Earth Doesn't Need Purple People!"

It was only a small group, and they were being held

Farewell to Earth

on the far side of the street by a line of police officers. Even so, it was distressing. I mean, can you imagine what it's like to know there are people you've never even met who dislike you so much that they want to throw you off their planet?

"Geez Louise, I thought we were done with this nonsense," said McNally. (That's what he prefers to be called. No "Mr." No first name. "Just McNally," he always says — which has led Shhh-foop, our Queen of the Kitchen, to think "Just McNally" is his name.)

Someone shouted a rude remark.

McNally shook his head in one of those Earthling gestures I find so interesting, then opened the door of the long black limousine we use to travel back and forth to and from the embassy.

The limo is heavily shielded against attack. I found this idea shocking when we first moved here. However, as time went on, I became increasingly glad to have this protection.

Ralph-the-Driver nodded as we took our places. He didn't say anything. He never did.

Suddenly one of the Earthling vegetables called a "tomato" splattered against the window.

A cheer broke out from the mob. The police began shouting and pushing them back.

"Drive!" ordered McNally.

Ralph nodded, and the limo moved swiftly away from the school.

Behind us I could hear the angry shouts of the mob.

Clearly, something very bad was going on.

But what was it?

CHAPTER 3

[TIM]
SLUDGED!

Rafaella and I watched in disgust as people shouted and shook their fists at the departing limo.

"All right, that's it," I said. "Something very weird is going on, and it's time we figured out what it is."

"Got any suggestions?" Rafaella asked. "It's not like the kids in class who are upset are willing to say anything. In fact, they act kind of scared."

I thought about that for a minute. "It's not just the kids in class. Whatever's going on, it's clear a bunch of people know about it. Otherwise we wouldn't have this mob outside school."

"But it's not something that's been on the news,"

continued Rafaella slowly, "because if it had been, we'd know about it too."

"So it's some kind of rumor," I said.

"And the best place to check out a rumor . . . ," said Rafaella.

"Is the Internet!" I smiled. "I think it's time we did some Net-surfing."

"Want to come to my house?" Rafaella asked.

I can't explain the feeling that hit my stomach at that moment. It was a strange mix of excitement and panic, horror and delight.

Rafaella is always nice to me, so I don't know why I feel so weird around her sometimes.

I figured the reason she invited me over was that she knows I don't have a computer of my own. I don't mean I don't have one in my room. I mean we don't even have one in the house. Mom claims we can't afford one. This is driving me nuts, since I think I'm the only kid in our class who *doesn't* have one at home.

Mom does not believe that. She can be very out of touch with reality sometimes.

I realized Rafaella was waiting for an answer.

"Let's go to the library," I said. "That way we can

Farewell to Earth

both get on computers and run two searches at once."

We're lucky. The library near us has a good computer system — though it almost got a lot less useful last year when a bunch of people tried to shut down Internet usage because they were afraid kids would see dirty pictures or something.

You'd think with kids starving to death and stuff like that, they would have more important things to worry about.

Once we got to the library, I spent a few minutes trying to figure out how to run my search. Just going for "aliens" would obviously turn up more hits than I could sift through.

I tried "alien rumors" and got about fifty matches that were all the same, for some stupid comic book.

I hate it when people do that.

I tried "alien abductions" with no better results. Just as I was starting to get frustrated, Rafaella said, "I think I've found something!"

"What?"

"Come here and take a look."

I went to stand behind her. "Oh, geez," I muttered.

She had pulled up the Sludge Report, an all-news/ all-gossip website run by this guy named Mort Sludge who is rabidly anti-alien. At the end of May he had also started a radio show. I'd heard it a couple of times when I was in the car with Mom. Even the guy's voice gave me the creeps.

He had posted a new item that day, under the category "Alien Treachery?"

Reading the article made me want to vomit.

Even so, we printed it out, since we thought we might need it.

Here it is:

What Happened to Linnsy Vanderhof?

That's the question being asked by parents whose children attend the school in Syracuse, NY, where Pleskit Meenom, Earth's only purple sixth grader, was forcibly installed by government authorities earlier this year.

Farewell to Earth

According to inside reports obtained by this source, the school has suffered one disaster after another since Pleskit's arrival. The most troubling situation occurred after Pleskit and two of his classmates, Tim Tompkins and Linnsy Vanderhof, disappeared from an event at the embassy. Though Tompkins and Pleskit eventually returned, young Linnsy was not with them.

Recently rumors have begun spreading in the anti-alien underground that she has been abducted—or worse—by hostile aliens.

Despite repeated inquiries from this reporter, the school has refused all comment.

Vanderhof's parents were not available. Some sources are whispering that the aliens have bought their silence.

So much for parental devotion.

The big question, of course, is: What has happened to an innocent sixth-grade girl who fell into the hands of these evil invaders?

This story is set to break nationally sometime in the next week. Fears that the whole purpose of the Hevi-Hevian mission is to kidnap Earth women are continuing to build in the anti-alien movement.

Developing . . .

CHAPTER 4

[PLESKIT]
VISITOR

I thought we were finished with protesters when we left the school. But as we drove up to the Hevi-Hevian embassy — which is also my home — I saw that demonstrators had gathered here as well.

"Is no place safe from this kind of thing?" I asked.

"'Fraid not," said McNally with a sigh.

The embassy is situated in a lovely green area called Thorncraft Park, which is quite peaceful when there are no demonstrations going on. The building itself dangles from a two-hundred-foot-tall metal hook that we inserted into the top of the hill. According to Tim, it looks like a flying saucer captured and put on display.

Guests who approach on foot (or by bicycle, as Tim often does) enter the embassy through a transport capsule housed in a small guard shack about fifty yards from the base of the hook. Those coming by car— mostly kings, queens, presidents, prime ministers, diplomats, and so on—enter through an underground garage. When an approved vehicle (such as the limo) gets close, a door opens in the side of the hill and we drive in, going down a long ramp to a garage located deep underground.

The garage has space for several cars besides the limo, plus a workbench for Ralph, and a small room with big windows that is both his office and resting place. The windows seem pretty useless, since the only thing he can see through them is the inside of the garage. I suspect they are there so he won't feel too cooped up.

When we approached home this afternoon, I saw something that was both exciting and frightening. Docked underneath the huge disk of the embassy was a small spaceship. We do not get visitors from off-planet terribly often. When we do, it usually portends something big happening.

Farewell to Earth

McNally and I rode the glass elevator up the hook, leaving Ralph in the garage to do . . . well, whatever Ralph-like things he does when he's not driving the limo. As usual, we went to the kitchen for a snack. Barvgis, the Fatherly One's slimeball assistant, was there already.

Earthlings tend to use the word "slimeball" for someone who is very nasty. This is not so for Barvgis. He is one of the nicest beings I have ever met. It is just that he is quite round, and quite slimy. It was not surprising to find him in the kitchen; it is his favorite place in the embassy.

Most of the rest of the embassy family was there, too, which was not so typical. Actually, except for the Grandfatherly One, whose brain (which is all we have left of him) was sitting at one end of the table in its portable transport device, they're not truly family. But when you are one of only a handful of off-worlders on a strange new planet, you tend to become very close to the people you live with.

Still, the fact that so many of them were here now, combined with the spaceship docked beneath the embassy, indicated that something was up.

Before I could figure out the best way to ask what was going on, Shhh-foop came sliding over to the table. She held a steaming pot in four of her orange tentacles. Another tentacle clutched a clear purple mug. "Some coffee for the handsome Just McNally?" she warbled.

A flicker of terror twitched across McNally's face. He is a brave man, as he has proved many times, but Shhh-foop's attempts to make this Earthly beverage have not been entirely successful. However, my body-guard is as kind as he is brave, so he smiled and said, "Sure, I'll give it a try, Shhh-foop."

Our Queen of the Kitchen hummed happily to herself as she poured the fragrant black liquid into the mug. Turning to me, she sang, "And how about you, my little Pleskit-pie? Would you like a snack? Some *febril gnurxis*? A plate of *finnikle-pokta*? I made some just for you."

Usually I have *febril gnurxis* after school; I love its crunchy sweetness. But Shhh-foop doesn't make *finnikle-pokta* that often, and the way the brightly colored nuggets jump around when you try to eat them amuses me. So I asked for those instead.

The Fatherly One's secretary, Beezle Whompis, had flickered out of sight. Because he is an energy being, it is not easy for him to hold a physical shape, and he

Farewell to Earth

really only does it as a courtesy to the rest of us. Now he crackled back into sight. His lean, blue face and deep-set eyes give him a serious, almost tragic look. Even so, I thought I saw a hint of mischief in those eyes as he said, "Aren't you going to try your coffee, McNally?"

"I'm waiting for it to cool down a bit," said McNally, giving him a cranky look.

Wakkam Akkim, the short, birdlike being who is the Fatherly One's spiritual massage-master, warbled a few notes — her way of saying, "Now, boys, let's not fight."

Shhh-foop slid back to the table with my *finnikle-pokta*. They were squeaking and rolling all over the plate, which had a kind of fence around it to keep them from escaping.

"Yikes!" cried Ronald the mutant hamster, who was sitting in a little chair set on the end of the table. Like the evil Doris, Ronald used to live in a cage in our classroom. But unlike Doris, Ronald had asked to come stay with us after his mutation. He seems to be getting comfortable with his new home, but he is still occasionally startled by Shhh-foop's cooking.

Our Queen of the Kitchen placed the lively little snacks in front of me, then turned and sang eagerly,

"How is the nectar of the caffeine bean, Just McNally?"

McNally sighed and lifted the steaming cup to his lips.

He took a sip.

He closed his eyes.

Shhh-foop watched anxiously, twisting her tentacles together as if her entire happiness depended on his approval.

McNally opened his mouth to speak — but no words came out. His eyes widened in surprise.

He tried again.

Nothing.

"*Ai-yi-yi-yikkle-demonga!*" wailed Shhh-foop operatically. "I have muted McNally!"

McNally pushed away from the table and stood up. He was pointing at his throat and waving his hands.

"What did you put in that stuff, Shhh-foop?" asked the Grandfatherly One.

"I added a pinch of *floogrot* from Ploodangi," she sang, tears dripping from the ends of her tentacles. "I thought it might make the coffee more tasty for the handsome Just McNally."

Just then the Fatherly One came into the kitchen.

Farewell to Earth

It was moderately surprising to see him, since he does not often join us. Even more surprising was the tall, orange-skinned being standing next to him: Sookutan Krimble, relative/mentor of the little pest Beebo who had caused Tim and me so much trouble in the past. At least now I knew who owned the small ship we had seen docked under the embassy.

In addition to being Beebo's relative/mentor, *Frek* Krimble is a high official in the Interplanetary Trading Federation. *Yeeble* is also a bit of a rebel and is part of a coalition working to improve the way the Federation treats minor planets such as Earth. *Yeeble* had been meeting with the Fatherly One fairly often over the last few weeks, but I did not know if *yeeble*'s presence now was good news or bad. I wondered if *yeeble*'s always arriving in a different ship indicated that *yeeble* was very important— or that *yeeble* was trying to disguise *yeeble*'s visits. What I wondered even more was what *yeeble* and the Fatherly One were up to.

When the two of them entered the kitchen, McNally turned and nodded a greeting. I could tell he was trying to act normal, so as not to get Shhh-foop in trouble.

The Fatherly One looked at McNally oddly but didn't comment. Turning to me, he said, "Pleskit, I need to speak to you. Please bring your Grandfatherly One as well."

He turned and left the room.

"Uh-oh," said the Grandfatherly One.

"What's the matter?" I asked. "I thought you were dying — excuse me, that was insensitive. I thought you were *eager* for the Fatherly One to consult you."

"I am. But given how long he's been ignoring me, if

he wants me in on this conference, it must be big stuff."

I turned to McNally. "I hate to leave you at this moment."

He shook his head and waved his hands, telling me not to worry. To my surprise, he was smiling.

Barvgis stepped up next to him and said, "I will take him to the Heal-a-tron and see if we can do anything to correct the situation."

Feeling slightly better, I lifted the Grandfatherly One's Brain Transport Device from the table and headed for the Fatherly One's office.

Behind me I could hear the wails of Shhh-foop, which had momentarily ceased when the Fatherly One had come into the kitchen.

From McNally, of course, I heard nothing at all.

CHAPTER 5

[TIM]
ME AND MY BIG MOUTH

That night I told my mother about the Sludge column while we were finishing dinner.

"Well, it's no surprise," she said.

"You mean because he's such a skeezeball?" I asked as I carried my plate to the counter.

Mom laughed. "Mort Sludge *is* a sleazy rumormonger. And he's mindlessly anti-alien. But in this case he had a seed to work with. After all, Linnsy *did* disappear."

"Sure, but there was no big deal about it. It was her choice to go off with Bur. She could have come back to Earth if she had wanted to."

Actually, Linnsy's not coming back was sort of a

24

Farewell to Earth

big deal for me personally, since she had been my official upstairs neighbor and my unofficial social adviser. And my friend. We'd known each other since we were in kindergarten, and I really missed her. Not to mention that I was slightly jealous of her being off exploring the galaxy while I was still stuck in sixth grade.

"You can say it's no big deal because you know the whole story," said Mom, starting to clear the table. "And if you and Pleskit ever publish that book you've been working on about what happened while you were off on that other planet, then everyone else will know too."

She stopped for a moment, and I could tell she was trying not to lose control. The weeks when Pleskit, Maktel, Linnsy, and I had been missing on Billa Kindikan — a planet we had gone to by complete accident — had been hard on her, and she still cried sometimes when she thought about that time. Turning to the sink to scrape a plate, she said, "The thing is, we all kept the story to ourselves. So for someone who has a conspiracy-oriented mind —"

"Like Mort Sludge," I said, starting to understand.

"Like Mort Sludge," agreed Mom, "that very silence is suspicious."

"But why is this happening now?" I asked. "It's been a couple of months since we came back."

"Well, rumors are a little like mushrooms."

I made a face. "I wouldn't want a rumor on my pizza!"

Mom laughed. "Neither would I. What I was talking about is the way that mushrooms have of popping up overnight."

"Yeah, what's with that, anyway?"

"Well, they don't really come out of nowhere. What happens is that the roots — or whatever they are — grow underground, out of sight, for a long time. Then, when the conditions are right, the mushroom suddenly appears. But it hasn't come out of nowhere. It's been building in the dark. That happens with rumors, too." She sighed. "I suppose we all helped create the darkness for this particular rumor to grow in by not talking about what happened."

The reason none of us had talked to the press about the whole thing was that Linnsy's parents didn't particularly want people to know their daughter was locked in a symbiotic union with a crablike creature named Bur, who was living on her head.

When we'd first met Bur, it had been attached to an

elegant, blue-skinned Trader named Ellico, and their full name was Ellico *vec* Bur. (The *vec* in a name indicates that two beings are linked in a symbiotic unit.) After Ellico died saving our lives on Billa Kindikan, Bur attached itself to Linnsy's head, which was when they became Linnsy *vec* Bur. In the beginning, Linnsy accepted the connection because we needed Bur's help to survive. But when the adventure was over, she chose to stay a *veccir*.

It's a good partnership, I suppose: Linnsy provides a strong, active body, and Bur provides a tremendously powerful brain that links with hers through a pair of *tweezikkle* hooked into Linnsy's ears. I once thought of saying to Mrs. Vanderhof, "Don't think of it as losing a daughter; think of it as gaining a brilliant space creature."

Fortunately, my mother talked me out of it.

"This kind of exploding rumor thing happens over and over again in politics," continued Mom as we started to load the dishwasher. "Some public figure does something embarrassing, tries to keep it secret, and ends up creating a far bigger fuss than he or she would have if they had just fessed up to begin with."

"Too bad the Vanderhofs aren't around to give Sludge a piece of their minds," I said.

Mom sighed. "I think I would have done the same thing if I were them."

What the Vanderhofs had done was disappear. They came downstairs one night and asked us to water their plants because they were going to go away for a while.

"Being at home makes me think of Linnsy too much," Mrs. Vanderhof had said, sniffing into a soggy handkerchief.

I knew what she meant, and it was all I could do to keep from bawling myself when I saw her like that.

Mr. Vanderhof didn't say anything, but his eyes had a sad, haunted look.

They didn't want to say where they were going, though I think Mom secretly knew. But since they weren't around now to straighten Sludge out, someone else had to do it.

Which was why I went back to the library that night and wrote this email:

Dear Mort Sludge,

My name is Tim Tompkins. I go to the same school as Pleskit Meenom, so I know him pretty well, and I wanted to tell you that you are all wrong when you talk about something terrible having happened to Linnsy Vanderhof.

Linnsy used to be one of my best friends. She is not dead. She has become part of an alien entity called a *veccir*, and she is off exploring outer space. Her parents don't want to talk about it, because they are a little embarrassed is all.

I think you should get your facts straight before you put things like that on the Internet. You could get some people very confused.

Also, since I am writing to you, I wanted to tell you that Pleskit and his Fatherly One are really good people. I don't know why you are so anti-alien, but I think it is a big mistake.

Ambassador Meenom's mission is more important to Earth than you can imagine.

Sincerely,

Tim Tompkins

Sludge wasn't the only one who had made a big mistake.

I had too.

My mistake, of course, was writing that letter—as I discovered all too soon.

CHAPTER 6

[PLESKIT]
FATEFUL MEETING

"Well, this should be interesting," said the Grandfatherly One as I carried his brain toward the Fatherly One's office.

"My life has been entirely too interesting since we arrived on Earth," I said.

"And my death has been entirely too dull since we got here," retorted the Grandfatherly One. "Despite your Fatherly One's claim that he kept me around after my death for the sake of my advice and wisdom, he has almost completely ignored me."

"You're the one who raised him," I said.

Farewell to Earth

"We all make mistakes," muttered my venerated ancestor.

Then we were at the office.

Beezle Whompis was already there, even though he had been in the kitchen when we'd left it. He can move very rapidly in his energy form. He crackled into sight and said, "You can go right in, Pleskit. Your Fatherly One and *Frek* Krimble are waiting for you."

The Fatherly One asked us to go into the Alcove of Intimacy, a small private room at the back of his office. Once we were there, he adjusted the table so that it was just the right size for the four of us—three of us in chairs and the Grandfatherly One's Brain Transport Device sitting between me and Sookutan Krimble.

"How is Beebo?" I asked, wondering if he was what this whole meeting was about.

The tips of *Frek* Krimble's ears twitched. I was not sure if this was a sign of amusement or agitation. "My *kribbl-pam* is his usual mischievous self. He sends his greetings. I would have brought him along, but this trip is too serious for the likes of him. Besides, he is being punished at the moment for a recent rather large-scale prank."

"Please give him my regards when you see him," I said.

Frek Krimble nodded in reply.

I was still wondering what this meeting was all about.

The Fatherly One folded his hands in front of him. "Pleskit, our mission on Earth is at a perilous moment," he said. "The discovery of the second Grand *Urpelli* within our franchise has the entire Trading Federation in an uproar. Many Traders are complaining that the prize is too rich for a single Trader to manage. Others—a smaller number than I would have thought, alas—are saying that I gained control of the *urpelli* under a standard contract, and it is not proper to change the rules just because the deal turned out to be bigger than anyone could have guessed."

"Bigger than anyone could have guessed" was a bit of an understatement. There are only two known Grand *Urpellis* in the galaxy, and they are incredibly valuable as transit points for interstellar travel. In fact, without them, interstellar travel would not be possible.

The second Grand *Urpelli*, which was unknown until a few months ago, has been dubbed "Gurp Two" for short. What made it so important to us was the fact

Farewell to Earth

that it happens to be within the bounds of our trading franchise — which meant the Fatherly One was in line to become the richest Trader in the galaxy!

Naturally, many other beings are dying to get their hands on this treasure, which is one reason we have had so many problems since our arrival on Earth. If our mission should fail, the Fatherly One's claim on this vast source of wealth would be invalidated and someone else would take it over.

I think it is exciting that we could become incredibly rich. On the other hand, I'm not sure the fuss is worth it. We had a good life before. Now I hardly ever see the Fatherly One, and even when I do, he is often distracted and cranky.

What good is all that money if it turns him into a *forzle*?

"The leaders of the Trading Federation will soon meet to decide what to do about this," said *Frek Krimble*. "I have agreed to advise your Fatherly One during this difficult time."

"Thank you for informing me of all this," I said.

"And for telling me," added the Grandfatherly One. "It's nice to be let in on things once in a while."

"There are two other things we need to let you in on," said the Fatherly One. "The first is our need to keep the situation here on Earth as smooth as possible. The last thing we need right now is any uproar or disruption. I am particularly concerned about the Helmscott Faction."

"What's that?" I asked.

Frek Krimble scowled. "The Helmscott Faction is a group of Traders that walks a little too close to the sneaky side of things. I believe they are working hard to undermine your position here — which is why you *must* avoid anything your rivals could use to try to convince the judges in Traders' Court that the franchise is being badly administered."

"Don't look at *me*," said the Grandfatherly One. "I couldn't cause trouble if I wanted to."

This was clearly a reference to the many unfortunate episodes Tim and I have experienced. While I love the Grandfatherly One, there are times when I would like to tie a knot in his speaking tubes.

"And the second thing?" I asked, eager to change the subject.

"It is something I have spoken of to you before," said

Farewell to Earth

the Fatherly One, looking troubled. "We are increasingly concerned that there is a traitor on the staff."

This sent a shiver of fear down my back — and also made a knot in my *gnorzle*. I am fond of everyone in the embassy, and I hated the idea of discovering that one of them was disloyal.

Actually, that's not entirely true. I wasn't at all fond of Ms. Buttsman, our protocol officer. But even she did not seem the type to be a traitor.

"Our fate — and the fate of Earth — is hanging by a thread," concluded the Fatherly One. "I just wanted you to know."

I was not sure that I felt the same way — that is, I was not sure that I wanted to know anything that big.

Actually, our own fate wasn't that big a deal. Even if we lost the franchise, we would not starve or anything. The Fatherly One is highly respected and would find work of one sort or another. But it could mean terrible things for Earth. What most people on the planet do not realize is that because they still have wars and other forms of stupidity, their world is not classified as civilized — which means there are very few restrictions on whoever controls the franchise. A Trader or Trade

35

Combine less ethical than the Fatherly One might try to squeeze the planet dry without trying to help the inhabitants.

When I remembered that, I thought maybe it was just as well that the Fatherly One was working so hard to keep the franchise.

Still, I would have liked our life to go back to what it was before we had the chance at this ridiculous wealth.

I didn't say any of this, of course. It was not appropriate to speak it with *Frek* Krimble in the room.

A few moments later the Fatherly One excused me.

I picked up the Grandfatherly One's Brain Transport Device and began to trudge back to his room.

McNally met us in the hall.

"Can you talk yet?" I asked eagerly.

"Just barely," he whispered, in a voice so soft that it sounded like *corrissmus*. "It's coming back slowly."

"Does it hurt?" I asked in concern.

McNally shook his head. "It just feels kind of numb. *Wakkam* Akkim says she thinks it will be fine by morning."

"That is a relief," I said. I looked at him more closely. "Why are you smiling?" I asked.

McNally's grin widened. "That was the best cup of

Farewell to Earth

coffee I ever had! I'm going to tell Shhh-foop right now. Of course, I can't drink any more of the stuff, unless I'm willing to be silent for an hour or so afterward. But I think it might be worth it. Man, that was good coffee!"

I watched with affection as my bodyguard headed for the kitchen. He has become very important to me.

A moment later we heard Shhh-foop warbling in delight.

The Grandfatherly One and I laughed and continued to the room where we keep his brain vat.

"Don't worry, sproutling," said my venerated ancestor after I had used the exchanger to return his brain to the main vat. "Even if the Trading Federation does recall us, it's not the end of the world."

"Not the end of *our* world," I said. "But what about the Earthlings?"

"Earthlings," he snorted. "What have they done for you?"

"Some of them have made me their friend," I said softly.

The Grandfatherly One sighed through his speaking tubes. "You shame me, sproutling. You're right. We need to protect them."

CHAPTER 7

[RAFAELLA]
A DEMONSTRATION OF STUPIDITY

I was sitting in the living room, fooling around with Gort, one of my pet king snakes. My father was watching *Hernando Rivers at Eight*, a news show he tunes in to so faithfully, you'd think it was a religion. Usually I ignore it, but suddenly Rivers said something that caught my attention.

"New rumors are swirling on the Internet about the controversial Hevi-Hevian embassy. The Sludge Report, which has become known for breaking stories with less evidence than mainstream news requires, claims that Linnsy Vanderhof, a sixth-grade girl who used to attend the same class as Pleskit Meenom, son of the alien

Farewell to Earth

ambassador, Meenom Ventrah, has mysteriously disappeared. Despite our requests, there has been no statement from the embassy or the school. We as yet have no confirmation of the story, which we'll continue to cover."

I stood up so fast that Gort had to do a couple of rapid twists to keep from falling off my hand. "That's disgusting!" I shouted.

"What?" asked my father, sounding surprised.

"Rivers doesn't have a story. He doesn't have any facts. He's just saying that someone else has said there might be a story. How can he do that? Anyone can say something *might* have happened. If that's all you need to call something news, you can put *anything* out there."

Dad looked a little embarrassed, and I remembered

that my mother sometimes called *Hernando Rivers at Eight* one of his guilty pleasures. "You're right," he said after a moment. Then, looking a little sterner, he said, "I only listen to Rivers so I can find out what people are saying."

"Oh, nonsense," said Uncle Alonso, who was sitting in the corner carving a turtle out of wood. "It's important to get out the truth about the aliens. If it weren't for people like Rivers and Mort Sludge, no one would have any idea what's going on with those evil creatures."

Uncle Alonso — he's really my great-uncle — has lived with us for the last three years, ever since Aunt Sophia died. He's very cranky, and he hates the aliens. So as soon as he said that, I knew there was going to be real trouble, because it was clear that he believed the rumors, despite the lack of any evidence. And if he believed them, a lot of other anti-alien nuts were also going to believe them.

I put Gort back in his cage, then went to the phone and called Tim.

"It's gone national," I said as soon as he answered.

"What do you mean?"

"I just saw Hernando Rivers doing a report on the rumors about Linnsy being abducted."

Tim groaned. "That's terrible! Now everyone else is

going to start reporting on Rivers's report. It will be in all the papers. And the reporters are going to be all over us."

I knew exactly what he meant. When Pleskit first moved here, reporters were constantly calling everyone in our class, trying to get inside stories. They did this despite the school having asked them not to. Some of them had even tried sneaking into the school — including one named Brianna who had actually gotten away with disguising herself as a kid for a little while.

All that had calmed down over the last several months as people had gotten used to the aliens being here. Syracuse was still crawling with reporters, of course — the aliens remained big news, if not the top story. But in the same way that Earth had gotten used to the aliens, we Syracusans had gotten used to the reporters, and after a while they'd mostly left us kids alone.

Clearly that was about to end.

If I had had any doubts about that fact, they vanished when I hung up from my conversation with Tim. The phone rang the instant I set it down.

I picked it up.

"Casa de Martinez," I said, which is the way we always answer the phone.

"Hi," said a cheerful voice. "This is Kitty James. Can I speak to Rafaella, please?"

I sighed. Kitty James had caused a lot of trouble during Pleskit's first week by making an inaccurate report about what had happened when Pleskit zapped Jordan with his *sphen-gnut-ksher* and put him into a dreamy kind of trance state called *kling-kphut*.

"This is Rafaella," I said.

"Oh, great! Listen, Rafaella, I was wondering if you could tell me anything about the Linnsy Vanderhof story."

"There's no story!" I shouted.

Then I hung up.

Actually, there was a story. But the Vanderhofs had asked us all not to talk about it, and I was going to honor their request— even if I was beginning to wonder if it had been a mistake.

Kitty was only the first of the reporters to call that night.

At eight thirty Mom took the phone off the hook.

The next day the demonstration outside the school was bigger and louder than before. Fortunately, the police

Farewell to Earth

were keeping the protesters well back from the school entrance.

Things were tense in class. Even though Pleskit and Tim had told all of us what had happened with Linnsy, I could sense that some of the kids no longer believed their story and were starting to wonder if Linnsy really had been abducted.

Three kids were absent. I had a feeling it was because their parents had kept them home.

Pleskit acted gloomy and unhappy all day and didn't raise his hand even once in class. (Usually he's full of both questions and answers.)

When we went outside for the daily run-around, I said, "Cheer up, Pleskit. It's just a bunch of people being idiots. They'll get over it."

"I'm not so sure," he said. "This is getting pretty serious. Can you come over to the embassy for a while this afternoon? You too, Tim."

We both accepted, of course. It would never occur to me not to. But when I told Misty Longacres that I was going to the embassy, she looked at me as if I had lost my mind.

"Are you crazy?" she cried. "I wouldn't go back to

that place for a million bucks! We still don't know what happened to Linnsy!"

I rolled my eyes and walked away.

I was planning to meet Tim outside the embassy. However, this plan got complicated by the fact that there was a huge crowd of demonstrators there. The police were holding them back, but there were a lot more demonstrators than there were police. When I showed my ID, the cops let me pass, but the crowd went nuts. Some started screaming and booing as if I were one of the bad guys on World Wrestling Entertainment. Others wanted to protect me from my own foolishness. *"Stop her!"* they screamed at the cops. *"That place isn't safe for Earth girls!"*

That was actually the least offensive thing the demonstrators said. Some of them were shouting — shrieking, really — horrible warnings about the things that would happen to me if I went inside the embassy.

I was fed up with this kind of stupidity. "Shut up!" I shouted. "You don't know anything about it."

One of the women dropped her sign and lunged at me, breaking through the police line as she did.

CHAPTER 8

[PLESKIT]
PROTECTION . . . OR PUNISHMENT?

It had been a hard day at school. The whis-pers and the finger-pointing were worse than ever. The class was now clearly divided into those who were talking to me and those who weren't. Ms. Weintraub looked hassled and harried and even yelled at us once, something she almost never does.

As for me, I was so caught up in my worries about the conversation I had had with the Fatherly One and *Frek* Krimble that I might as well have been sealed in a box for all the learning I did.

The only good thing that happened during the day was that Tim and Rafaella agreed to come to the embassy for a visit that afternoon — though even that was fraught with tension for me, since I felt I had to tell them how bad things were getting. Even so, I was relieved when the day was over. I was looking forward to the peace and quiet of home. But just as McNally and I were leaving, Ms. Weintraub said, "Pleskit, can you stay for a few minutes?"

It turned out she wanted to talk to me about what was going on. Mostly it was apologies for the way the kids, not to mention the world, were behaving. I appreciated the thought, but at that time I mostly wanted to get home, especially since Tim and Rafaella were coming over.

When we drove into Thorncraft Park, I could hear — even before I saw it — a demonstration going on here as well.

I sank back against the seat. "Maybe we *should* give up and go back to Hevi-Hevi," I said in despair.

"Quitting gets you nowhere," said McNally grimly. His jaw was set, his expression angry. I didn't understand why his reaction was so fierce until I remembered that only sixty years ago people of his color had had to face mobs like this in our host

Farewell to Earth

country simply because they wanted the right to go to the same schools as the white children. (If you ask me, "white" is a strange term to use for people who are a variety of shades of pink and tan. But, like many things about this planet, Earthling feelings

about skin color do not make total sense to a civilized being.)

As we got closer to the embassy, we saw that the
crowd was bigger and rowdier than any since our first
few weeks on the planet.

"Take it easy, Ralph," said McNally. "And be ready to
back up if I give the word."

Ralph nodded.

We drove forward slowly.

Suddenly we heard a commotion off to the right.
Looking over, I saw Rafaella trying to make her way forward on her bike.

To my horror, someone broke through the police
line and grabbed her.

McNally uttered a curse word. "Stay here!" he
ordered. Springing out of the limo, he plunged into the
crowd and began plowing his way toward Rafaella.

"Alien lover!" shouted some of the people when
they saw him.

"Traitor to Earth!" shrieked someone else.

The police were struggling to hold the crowd back,
but a lot of the protesters had burst through the line.
People started to scream. I lost sight of McNally for a

moment. I could feel myself slipping toward *kleptra* and fought to stay alert.

Suddenly McNally was at the door of the limo. He had Rafaella clutched to his side.

I opened the door, and they slipped in. Hands were reaching toward them, and I could hear the police shouting for people to get back.

"Bumpers!" ordered McNally. "Fog!"

Ralph nodded and pushed a couple of buttons. Instantly padded bumpers thrust out of the sides of the limo, creating a protective ring around us. At the same time, we heard a hissing sound. Seconds later we were surrounded by a thick, gray mist.

"Wow!" said Rafaella. "I didn't know this thing could do *that!*"

"Neither did I," I said.

Ralph began backing up, moving slowly. We heard people shout and curse. Some stones struck the limo, but the windows were shatterproof. We continued to move, and the bumpers gently nudged people out of the way.

Once we were out of the park, McNally put in a call to the embassy to let them know we were going to be late.

"Tim's already inside," he told us after he closed the line. "He made it in with no problem."

That was a relief. I had been greatly worried about him.

"I probably should have kept my mouth shut," said Rafaella ruefully.

"Might have been smarter," said McNally with a nod. "But I like a woman who sticks up for what she believes in."

Rafaella smiled. I noticed that she was developing what the Earthlings call a black eye.

Half an hour later the police had the mob under control, and Ralph was able to drive up to the embassy. Most of the staff had gathered in the kitchen to wait for us, and they applauded when we came in. (Of course, applause is expressed in many different ways across the galaxy. Shhh-foop showed her approval by whirling her tentacles to create a whizzing sound, and Barvgis generated a string of musical belches.)

I appreciated their support, as did Rafaella once I had explained it to her.

"I can't believe you told that woman off, Rafaella,"

said Tim admiringly. "I didn't dare say a thing when I was coming past that mob."

The Fatherly One looked at her appraisingly for a moment, then said, "You may be able to help me, Rafaella."

She blinked in surprise. "How?"

He bent his *sphen-gnut-ksher* in a sign of discomfort, then said, "I have accepted an invitation to appear on television tomorrow to defend the mission. I will be confronting Mort Sludge directly to try to answer concerns about what we are doing. I was wondering if you would accompany me to the studio and appear on the show with me."

"I'd be glad to," said Rafaella. "But why?"

The Fatherly One smiled. "To be honest, given the Linnsy rumors, I think it will help our case to have a female from your class there to support me." He paused again, then said, "Do you think your parents would be interested in coming along as well?"

"They might be," said Rafaella. "Of course, Uncle Alonso will probably cut them out of his will if they do."

"For what reason?" asked Barvgis, who was playing with his squirmers instead of eating them — a sure sign that he was upset.

Rafaella looked uncomfortable. "Uncle Alonso is anti-alien. It's not easy living with him."

"Well, at least you know how they think," said *Wakkam* Akkim. "It is always good to understand the opposing force."

As if the day had not been full enough, after Rafaella and Tim had gone home and I'd had dinner, Ms. Buttsman announced that Principal Grand and Ms. Weintraub had arrived for a conference. Normally I would have figured this meant I had done something wrong and was in big trouble, but now I assumed it was about all the trouble being created by others.

I was partly right. The conference *was* about what was going on. But *I* was the one who was going to be punished for it.

Only, they didn't call it punishment.

They called it protection.

The three of them—the Fatherly One, the principal, and my teacher—met privately at first, the way grown-ups tend to do when they're going to drop something big on a kid. When they were done, they joined me in the Alcove of Intimacy, where I had been

Farewell to Earth

awaiting them, anxiously wondering what this was all about.

They sat down, looking grim and unhappy.

The Fatherly One spoke first. "Pleskit, we have made a decision. Until this crisis is over, we feel it would be wise to restrict you to the embassy."

"But I did not do anything wrong!" I protested.

"This isn't punishment for anything you've done, Pleskit," said Mr. Grand gently. "It's caution. It's simply not safe out there for you in the current climate."

"I've got McNally," I said, feeling desperate.

The Fatherly One emitted the acrid smell of negation. "Mr. McNally is on suspension."

"What?" I cried.

"This is not my decision," said the Fatherly One, lifting his hands. "Mr. McNally is an employee of our host government, and they have recalled him for the time being, because of his actions this afternoon."

"What actions?" I asked in shock.

"He left your side at a time of crisis."

"But he did it to help Rafaella!"

"I understand that," said the Fatherly One. "However, his obligation was not to protect Rafaella; it was to protect you. Leaving your side in that situation was a serious violation of his professional rules."

"Can't you ask to have him back?"

The Fatherly One bent his *sphen-gnut-ksher* sadly. "Since you will not be going to school for now, I would have a hard time making the case. Besides, I am also rather vexed with Mr. McNally for leaving you. I am not sure that I want him back."

I glanced at Ms. Weintraub, but her face had gone so still — hard, almost — that I could not tell what she was thinking. I wanted her to defend McNally, especially since I thought she kind of liked him. But she sat in stony silence.

Maybe it was guilt. I hoped so.

I trudged to my room. At the beginning of the year, I hadn't wanted to go to school and had been forced to.

Now I wanted to go and was being forced to stay home!

I know life isn't always fair, but this was getting ridiculous.

CHAPTER 9

[TIM]
BANISHED!

I had a bad feeling when Pleskit wasn't in school the next day. He's incredibly healthy and hadn't been out sick all year. (Advanced medicine is just one of the things the aliens have to offer us if Earth ever gets totally accepted into the Interplanetary Trading Federation.)

Between the distraction of the demonstrators and worry about Pleskit, I couldn't focus and kept making stupid mistakes. I expected Ms. Weintraub to yell at me, but she wasn't much better than I was. She seemed distracted and upset about something, and hardly even noticed when I messed up.

I wanted to ask her what was bothering her, since I figured it might have to do with all the alien uproar. But I didn't, partly because it might have been personal, partly because I didn't have a chance.

It was totally weird not to have Pleskit and McNally around all day. When it was time to go out for the run-around, I realized I was a little nervous because even though McNally was Pleskit's bodyguard and not mine, I always had the feeling that he intimidated Jordan a little and kept him from doing some of the worst stuff that he might try.

I know now that that wasn't entirely fair of me. Jordan had been acting different ever since we'd survived the revolt of the miniature mutants and the trip to the Monster Dimension together. But it's hard to suddenly change the way you feel about someone who's been your archenemy for the better (or worse) part of two years.

Anyway, Jordan wasn't my problem that day. I was. Or at least what I had done was, as I figured out when Misty Longacres came up to me and said, "Nice letter you sent to Mort Sludge, Tim."

"How do you know what I wrote to Sludge?" I asked, suddenly feeling nervous.

Farewell to Earth

"I read it on the Internet this morning."

I felt a sudden sick twist in my stomach. I had not meant for that letter to be published. It was just supposed to make Sludge think twice before he published stuff he couldn't prove.

Several other kids gathered around to tell me they had seen it too. They seemed more impressed with the idea that Sludge had published the letter than with what I had actually said in it.

Unfortunately, this would not turn out to be the case for everyone.

After school that day I didn't even hang around to talk to Rafaella. Instead I shot home as quickly as I could, so I could call Pleskit and see if he was all right.

When I got to the apartment, I didn't even stop in the kitchen but went straight to my room, plowing through the stuff on the floor to get to my desk. My Veeblax was there, trying to imitate a Lance Driscoll action figure. The result was kind of gross-looking, since the Veeblax is still young and can't do complicated shapes very well. Even so, I pretended to be surprised when it stuck out its eye stalks, which made it happy. It climbed onto my shoulder, then began making a contented thrumming sound in its throat that vibrated pleasantly against my neck.

I turned on the comm-device Pleskit had given me so we can see each other when we talk. (It has a component for transmitting odors, too, but I usually leave that off, since I can't really translate smells yet.)

He answered on the first buzz.

"I thought you might be calling," he said.

He looked terrible.

"What's going on?" I asked.

"Can you come over to the embassy?" he replied, which wasn't really an answer.

"You mean right now?" I asked, feeling a weird combination of excitement (I *love* going to the embassy) and dread (since Pleskit was obviously so upset).

"Yes."

"Well, Mom won't be home from work for another couple of hours. So it should be all right."

"Good. Come over as soon as you can. I'll explain everything then."

I couldn't get over there fast enough.

The demonstrators outside the embassy were louder than ever, but the number of police had increased too, and they were holding the mob farther back than before.

I had a little trouble getting past the police line, but about the time they were going to send me away, one of the guards came running up with a note saying that I was to be let through.

People screamed and yelled when they saw me going in.

"Traitor!" they cried. "Sellout!"

One woman, her face red, shouted, "Linnsy's blood is on your hands!"

Given the fact that I had saved Linnsy's life while we were on Billa Kindikan, that one really hurt.

I felt lousy—and wondered what it was like for Pleskit to have to go past those fanatics every day.

From the guard shack where I entered, you ride a silver and crimson capsule to get into the embassy itself. The ride is incredibly smooth, even though it only takes about ten seconds.

Pleskit was waiting for me when I climbed out of the capsule. He had his Veeblax on his shoulder, and it reminded me of the very first time I had come to visit.

Except this time they both looked incredibly gloomy.

"What's going on?" I said.

"Let's go to my room," he replied, which wasn't really an answer.

When we got there, he turned the lights down low, then did one of those weird Hevi-Hevian interpretive dances. This was a slow one, and had fewer farts than usual, though I have to say the last one was really a killer.

"The Dance of Parting," he said when he was done.

"*What?*" I cried.

"I'm not coming back to school, Tim. I've been Earthed!"

It took me a minute to figure out what he meant. "You've been grounded?" I cried when I finally got it. "What for? What did you do?"

He belched sorrowfully. "*Nothing!* That is the worst part of it. But McNally has been called away, as punishment for—"

"*What?*" I cried again, even more astonished and upset than before. "Who did it? And why?"

"Your government claims he neglected his duty by leaving my side to help Rafaella. The Fatherly One is

Farewell to Earth

not willing to contest their decision, because he has decided that school has become too dangerous, not simply for me but for our public relations."

He paused and looked away. When he turned back, he said, "Tim, there is a very good chance that the mission will be terminated within the next several days. I am very sorry. I did all I could to help make it work."

I couldn't believe what I was hearing. There had been a number of times when we'd thought the mission might be ending, but it had always been when we were in the middle of some life-threatening adventure. That it would just end quietly like this was hard to believe, especially when I thought about what it would mean for the planet if Meenom left and one of the other Traders — a Trader who didn't believe in helping a poor, uncivilized planet like ours — took over in his place.

Pleskit and I had a last bounce on his bed, which is this incredible mattress made out of "thick air" and controlled by a molecular shield. You can't see it, but it's better than a trampoline. We got laughing so hard that we finally fell off the edge. We lay there on the floor for a while, staring at the ceiling and not talking. Then he took me to see his Fatherly One.

Meenom was waiting for me, looking tired and sorrowful.

He was holding something. I realized with a sense of horror that it was a printout of Mort Sludge's column — the one that had my letter in it.

"Tim, did you really write this?" he said.

I wanted to deny it but couldn't. "It's mine," I admitted.

"Including the line 'Ambassador Meenom's mission is more important to Earth than you can imagine'?"

I nodded. "I was just trying to help when I —"

Meenom raised a hand to stop me. "I do not doubt your motives, Tim. But this has created enormous problems for me. The anti-alien crowd is taking it as a threat. The Traders monitoring the situation are pointing to it as a sign that the mission is out of control and that I am lax in my security."

I bowed my head. "I'm sorry, sir. I was just trying to help."

"I know that, Tim. And you do know, I hope, that I truly have Earth's best interests at heart."

Farewell to Earth

"I believe that completely," I said.

Meenom closed his eyes for a moment, then said, "Then I hope you will understand that it is not personal anger that leads me to this."

"To what?" I cried.

"I am banishing you from the embassy, Tim."

I felt a horrible coldness inside. I wanted to throw myself at his feet, clutch his knees, and beg for mercy, the way Beebo did when he got in trouble, but I felt as if I were frozen.

"I have to show that I am taking solid action on this matter, Tim. I'm sorry, but things are so delicate now that I don't have the room to maneuver, or ignore things, the way I might have even a month ago."

"I understand," I said.

At least, I tried to say it. My throat was so thick, I'm not sure the words actually made it out.

Pleskit put his arm around my shoulder and led me out of the office.

"I'm sorry," I kept whispering. "I'm sorry. I didn't mean to do anything wrong."

"I know," he said. "You are as good a friend as I have ever had."

When we got to the departure room, I almost burst into tears. The staff had gathered to say good-bye. I knew what this meant: they thought it was possible they would never see me again.

The only one not there was Ms. Buttsman, which did not surprise me.

The first to say his farewell was Barvgis — great, blubbery, lumbering Barvgis, who was always so kind and had never tired of practicing his Earth jokes on me. He took my hand in his, and the slimy feel of it didn't bother me at all.

Beezle Whompis couldn't take my hand, of course. He just stood there, all energy and crackle, flickering in and out of sight, his lean face looking even more doleful than usual. "Farewell, Tim," he said, his voice staticky with emotion. "I hope to see you again quite soon, but if I do not — well, it has been a privilege to know you."

Wakkam Akkim stepped up beside him. Her bird-like features, usually so serene, showed great sorrow. Leaning forward, she gave me a peck on the cheek. "Be wise," she whispered.

The Grandfatherly One, Ronald, even Eargon Fooz, the creature who had come back with us from Billa

Bruce Coville

Kindikan to wait out her year of exile, bid me a kind, sad farewell.

Last of all was Shhh-foop, dear Shhh-foop, who had stood singing tragically to herself, her tentacles twitching in sorrow, as she'd waited her turn.

"Be safe, be safe, oh brave little consumer of my cooking," she warbled. Taking my face in her tentacles, she bent forward and gave me a kiss on the forehead.

Then she turned and fled.

I entered the capsule that would take me back to the guard shack.

I'd been in worse danger.

But I'd never felt so much like my life was about to end.

CHAPTER 10

[JORDAN]
DETECTIVES

Okay, this is Jordan talking now. The last time I did a chapter for Tim and Pleskit, it was because Ms. Weintraub said she would give me some extra credit in English if I did.

This time it's because I have some things I need to get off my chest—things I don't want anyone else to tell. And it's going to take me more than one chapter to do it.

To begin with, I want to say right here that I didn't care what my mother said about Pleskit. I had decided he was pretty cool. So I was really upset when Rafaella called and said that Tim had told her our official alien wasn't coming back to school.

I didn't say anything about this at home, of course. It wasn't worth the trouble. But the next morning, as Tim was walking into school, I called him over to the corner where I usually hang out.

"Hey, Squeege-face," I said. "Come here. I want to talk to you for a minute."

The way he flinched, you would have thought I beat him up on a daily basis. So I want to make this clear right now: I have not beat him up once this year, and that's the truth.

So I don't know why he was so jumpy.

The other truth is that while Tim may be a totally dorky kid, he's been involved in more real action than anyone else I know, except maybe my grandfather, who was in Vietnam. Despite Tim's dorkitude, I think it's pretty cool how he keeps facing up to alien menaces and surviving.

Even so, I felt a little weird about being seen with him. I mean, I do have a reputation to uphold. And I had to tell Brad Kent to bug off, since I didn't think Tim could cope with both of us at once.

Tim came over, looking wide-eyed and edgy.

"Calm down," I said. "I'm not going to hurt you. I just want to talk to you."

Farewell to Earth

"About what?" he asked, cautiously stepping closer.

"Pleskit."

Immediately he looked alert, almost fierce. "What about him?"

"That's what I want to know. Why isn't he coming back to school?"

"His Fatherly One has pulled him out, for his own protection."

"Man, that stinks!"

Tim looked surprised, which made me want to hit him. I glanced around to make sure no one was close enough to hear me, then said, "This is about all that stuff getting leaked to the press, isn't it?"

Tim nodded. He had a really strange expression on his face.

"Okay," I said. "I think we'd better do something about it."

Tim looked even more surprised than before. "Do what?"

"I don't know. Some investigating. You know, like the Hardy Boys. Maybe we can figure out what's going on."

"Are you serious?"

I rolled my eyes. "Do you have to be such a dork? It would make things easier if you weren't."

Tim looked at me for a minute, then smiled. "Okay, let's do it," he said. "When do you want to start?"

"As soon as possible."

"How about today during the run-around?"

I hesitated. Even though I was willing to work with him on this, I still wasn't sure I actually wanted to be seen with him on the playground. "Let's make it after school," I suggested.

"Where?"

Now, this was a problem. I don't like to invite people to my house, none of your business why. But it seemed too weird to go to Tim's place.

While I was hesitating, he said, "Maybe we should bring Rafaella in on this."

That was fine with me. Rafaella is totally a babe.

"We might be able to get together at her house to work on it," added Tim.

Which solved that problem.

We were sitting in Rafaella's living room, drinking Cokes and playing with her snakes (Rafaella is totally

Farewell to Earth

cool!) while we tried to figure out what, if anything, we could do about the Pleskit situation. Except none of us seemed to have any ideas.

I was carrying Gort back to his cage when the phone rang. Rafaella picked it up, listened for a minute, then slammed it back down.

"Reporter?" asked Tim.

She nodded.

Made me glad we have an unlisted number.

Suddenly Tim sat up and cried, "Why didn't I think of this before? What about Brianna?"

I laughed out loud, which made him blush.

Brianna Sawyer was this very cute, very young-looking female reporter who had infiltrated our class toward the beginning of the year by pretending to be a sixth grader. Tim had been a little in love with her, which had been pretty funny to see — especially since he thought he had kept it hidden. On the other hand, he was the one who'd stopped Brianna when she'd tried to steal the brain of Pleskit's Grandfatherly One. So he obviously wasn't totally twitterpated.

"That's not a bad idea, Tim," said Rafaella. "There was always something a little shady about Brianna. I wouldn't be surprised if she's connected with all this."

I wondered if Rafaella had been jealous of the way Tim had felt about Brianna; then I pushed the idea out of my head. The thought that a babe like Rafaella might care about Tim was too weird for real life.

"But how do we get ahold of her?" said Tim, slumping back in his chair.

"That's no problem," said Rafaella. "She gave me her number back when she was in our class."

"And you still have it?" asked Tim in astonishment.

Rafaella laughed. "Not everyone is as disorganized as you are, Tim."

"Getting ahold of Brianna isn't the problem," I said. "How do we get her to talk to us?"

"Are you kidding?" said Rafaella. "Every reporter in the world wants to talk to kids from our school. All we do is tell her we want to talk to her, and she'll be knocking on the door before we can hang up the phone."

She went to her room and came back a minute later with a little blue book. "Here we go," she said.

She dialed the phone.

Brianna didn't show up quite as fast as Rafaella

had predicted. We had to wait almost fifteen minutes before she was ringing the doorbell.

It was pretty funny watching Tim's reaction when she showed up. He turned into this weird mixture of puppy and tough guy, and I wasn't sure if he was going to ask her for a kiss or slap her face.

"So, what do you three have to tell me?" asked Brianna, whipping a little tape recorder out of her purse.

"The question is, what do you have to tell us?" said Tim.

She scowled at him. "What are you talking about?"

"Look, Brianna," said Rafaella. "There's a lot of news getting leaked out of the embassy. We want to know where it's coming from. And we think you can tell us."

"What if I could?" she said defiantly. "I don't give away that kind of thing for nothing. I want some news in return."

At that point it turned into a standoff. We sure weren't going to give Brianna any more information about Pleskit and the embassy. And she didn't intend to tell us anything without a trade.

I decided it was time to step in.

"Give me your pad for a second," I said.

"What for?" asked Brianna.

"Just give it to me," I said, reaching out.

Brianna shrugged and handed it to me.

I wrote my father's name on it and handed it back to her.

Brianna's eyes widened. "Are you kidding?"

I took out my wallet and flipped it open to my ID card.

That did the trick. She licked her lips nervously, then said, "Look, I can't tell you much . . ." She paused and glanced around as if she thought there might be spies in the room or a hidden camera or something.

"Come on," I said threateningly. "Let's have it."

She took a deep breath, then gave us a name that made Tim gasp in surprise.

CHAPTER 11

[TIM]
SPYING

I was dying to know what Jordan had written on the pad he'd showed Brianna. But before I could ask, she gave us the information we wanted, and I thought my brain was going to short-circuit. I stared at her in astonishment. "You've got to be kidding," I said.

She glanced at Jordan, then shook her head. "Not kidding," she said. "Not worth it."

"You're telling us that *Ralph-the-Driver* is the leak?"

Brianna stood up. "If you don't want to believe me, I might as well leave right now."

"No, no, no," I said quickly. "I'm sorry. It's just . . . I didn't expect it."

"Ralph's been passing information to reporters from the beginning," said Brianna. "He's got a little transmitter in the limousine. Sometimes he turns it on so we can hear conversations that are happening in the car."

I remembered Pleskit telling me he had seen Ralph flip some switch that Pleskit had been curious about. Well, now we knew what it was.

"Frankly, I didn't get nearly as much information on the alien mission as I would have liked," said Brianna. She smiled viciously and added, "I did hear quite a bit about Tim's personal life. But that's not really newsworthy."

"You creep!" I cried.

"Who's in on this?"' asked Rafaella, which was more to the point.

"I don't know for sure," said Brianna. "I do know that I'm not the only one he passes the stuff on to. There are a lot of reporters getting his info."

"Who's paying him?" asked Jordan. Turning to me, he added, "My dad always says that if you want to figure out what's going on, follow the money."

It didn't surprise me that Jordan's father would say this.

Brianna shook her head. "I don't know."

Farewell to Earth

"All right," said Jordan, "then who pays *you*?"

She laughed bitterly. "At the moment, no one. I'm out of work."

I could see that Jordan was getting annoyed. "Well, who *was* paying you?" he persisted.

"The Boss."

Brianna had mentioned "the Boss" once before, after we had unveiled her as an impostor when she'd stolen the brain of Pleskit's Grandfatherly One. She hadn't known who it was then, and despite our questions and Jordan's threats, she claimed she didn't know now.

We asked her a few more questions, but it was clear she had told us all she knew, or at least all she was willing to tell.

"Okay," said Rafaella after Brianna was gone. "Now what do we do?"

"We should let Meenom know what's going on," said Jordan.

"Well, it sure won't be me who does that," I said glumly. "Meenom has banned me from the embassy."

"I can go in to talk to Pleskit," said Rafaella.

"Won't do much good," said Jordan.

"Why not?" I asked.

"Look, Meenom's not gonna believe us if we tell him some guy who's been working for him all year is a traitor— especially if all we have to go on is info we got from some out-of-work reporter. We need proof. We need to catch Ralph in the act."

"How are we supposed to do that?" I said. "It's not like we can get into the limo with him."

Jordan rolled his eyes. "I thought you were supposed to be the adventure guy," he said, sounding disgusted. "What we have to do is get into the garage area somehow and spy on Ralph. Then maybe we can catch him doing something suspicious. Or at least get a clue or something."

My first thought was that Jordan really had been reading too many Hardy Boys books. But the more I thought about it, the more I realized he was right about needing some proof.

"That really could work," I said, starting to get excited. "Maybe we could even get the transmitter out of the limo. That would be perfect for proof!"

"Okay, so how do we get into the garage?" said Jordan.

"Pleskit might be able to help us if Rafaella explains what's going on."

Farewell to Earth

"Why don't you?" said Jordan.

"I'm not allowed to talk to him," I said bitterly. "I had to send my comm-device back."

"Man, that stinks!" cried Jordan, with more sympathy than I would have expected.

"You're a victim of interplanetary politics, Tim," said Rafaella. "Fortunately, I can still call Pleskit on a regular line."

Hey, what can I say? It seemed like a good idea at the time.

It even pretty much worked, at least the first part of it. Rafaella made contact with Pleskit, who was shocked and horrified when she told him what we had learned about Ralph, and what we wanted to do. Though he was somewhat nervous about it, he agreed to help us out by getting visitor passes for her and Jordan. The big question was whether the guys who manned the guard shack had been told to keep me out, or if Meenom had simply figured that once I was banished, I would voluntarily stay away.

That would have been a fair assumption under normal circumstances. I don't like to go where I'm not wanted. But these were not normal circumstances.

Rafaella called me later that evening, all excited.

"Good news," she said. "You're on the honor system. Meenom didn't say anything to the guard shack crew. So we can get you in."

It made me kind of sick to think of breaking the banishment that way. But I wasn't really going to go visit Pleskit. I wasn't even really going to go into the embassy, at least not for any longer than it took me to get through it to the garage.

The next afternoon the three of us showed up at the guard shack. The guy on duty recognized me; he had let me in a hundred times before. And Rafaella and Jordan had their official pass for the day. So it was easy enough for us to get in.

Feeling guilty, I rode the capsule up to the embassy with them. Then Jordan and I peeled off and moved as quickly as we could to the main tube, which took us down to where the limo was kept.

No one saw us — not even Pleskit, who stayed away so that he wouldn't be breaking his Fatherly One's order.

That hurt, but I understood. We were on tricky ground now.

***

Farewell to Earth

"Okay, the coast is clear," said Jordan a few seconds after the elevator deposited the two of us in the garage. He was pressed against a wall and peering around the corner. "Ralph's in that little office thing with his face stuck in a newspaper. Stay down!"

I followed Jordan, crouching close to the wall, until we reached the hiding places we had picked out from a diagram of the garage that Pleskit had provided to Rafaella. The spots were about fifteen feet apart, one behind a stack of tires, the other behind a bench that held a bunch of tools for working on the limo.

This kind of waiting can be long and boring, and I was somewhat uncomfortable about Jordan being my partner for it. On the other hand, since we were hiding in separate spots and it was important for us to keep silent, at least he wouldn't be hassling me.

We had been there for about an hour when Rafaella slipped in beside me.

"What are you doing here?" I whispered in alarm.

"Shhh! I brought something for you to eat," she said, unwrapping a package of some of Shhh-foop's snacks.

"You shouldn't have come. It could be dangerous!"

"Oh, hush up and eat," she replied.

Since I had been starting to get pretty hungry, I decided to obey.

I was finishing up the last snack when Ralph came out of his little room. He looked around in a nervous kind of way, then took a small black device out of his pocket. He tapped on it a couple of times. A moment later a voice — not the voice of anyone in the embassy — came out of the device.

"Is that you, Driver?" it asked.

I glanced at Rafaella. Maybe this was it!

Then something horrible happened.

I hiccuped.

I knew I shouldn't have eaten that alien food!

Ralph spun around, looking startled and suspicious.

Rafaella clamped her hand over my mouth, but it did no good. Shhh-foop's snack had done something to my innards.

I hiccuped again.

Ralph turned in our direction.

Rafaella and I squinched against the wall, desperately hoping that he wouldn't be able to spot us. He had almost reached the bench when Jordan tossed a piece of something he had found onto the floor. It landed with

Farewell to Earth

a clink. Immediately Ralph spun in that direction.

For a moment, I thought we were safe.

Then I hiccuped again.

With a snarl — the first sound I had ever heard out of him — Ralph spun in our direction once more.

I looked at Rafaella crouching beside me and decided that I couldn't let him get her.

So I stood up. Trying to sound calm and casual, I stepped out from the hiding place. "Hey, Ralph," I said. "It's just me. Tim. I didn't mean to scare you. I know I shouldn't be here, but I wanted to talk to you for a minute."

I started toward him, hoping to lead his eye away from where Rafaella was still hiding.

"I was hoping —"

I stopped. Ralph was looming over me. He didn't say a word, but he looked incredibly menacing. His eyes were furious.

I took a step back.

He came toward me.

"Back off, buddy," said a voice from behind me.

It was Jordan.

A second later I was astonished to see him standing next to me.

Bruce Coville

Obviously, Ralph didn't find Jordan as intimidating as I did. He didn't back off.

Instead he took out a purple ray gun and pointed it at us.

"I've been waiting a long time for this," he said.

They were the first words I ever heard him speak. Yet, to my astonishment, his voice sounded familiar.

I didn't have time to think about that, because he pulled the trigger on the ray gun.

CHAPTER 12

[RAFAELLA]
DISASTER

I watched in terror as Ralph fired his ray gun, and a wave of purple light hit first Tim and then Jordan.

Side by side, they crumpled to the floor.

I wanted to rush in to save them, but I had nothing to use against Ralph, and I was sure that the moment I came out of hiding, he would zap me too. Then there would be no one to take word of what had happened up to the embassy.

So I stayed crouched where I was. It felt cowardly, but I couldn't think of any better way to help the boys.

My stomach knotting and twisting, I watched Ralph load Tim and Jordan into the trunk of the limo. Then he climbed into the driver's seat and started the engine.

The instant the limo headed up the tunnel, I bolted out of my hiding place and raced for the elevator.

Seconds later I was back in the embassy.

I ran to the kitchen, where Pleskit had promised to wait for me. He was sitting there, looking nervous, while Shhh-foop slid around trying to entice him to eat.

"Pleskit!" I cried. "I have to talk to you!"

He excused himself and hurried out into the hall with me.

"What is it?" he asked. "Did you find out something? Where are Jordan and Tim?"

"Ralph kidnapped them!"

Pleskit let out the most horrible odor I had ever smelled, and for a second I thought he was going to fall over. But he grabbed his *sphen-gnut-ksher* and pulled it up straight, as if forcing himself to stay standing.

"We've got to tell your Fatherly One," I said.

Pleskit shook his head. "We can't. He's not here."

"Not here? But he's supposed to meet me at the studio today for that show with Mort Sludge." I glanced at my watch. "In less than two hours!"

"He'll be back in time for that," said Pleskit. "But

right now he's in the Middle East, having a meeting with some sheik or something. Oh, if only they hadn't taken McNally away from me."

"Well, we'll have to get someone else," I said. "What about Barvgis?"

"He's with the Fatherly One."

"Beezle Whompis?"

"The same."

"They all went off and left you?" I asked.

"Rafaella, I am old enough not to need a babysitter. Even if I did need one, Shhh-foop has a Galaxy One Child Care Certification. The embassy is well guarded and fortified with more protective devices than you can imagine—"

"All right, all right," I said. "I was just surprised. You don't need to justify it. But we have to figure out what to do. What about *Wakkam* Akkim?"

"She has gone to Tibet to meet with some holy men."

"Then let's just call the police!" I cried.

I had held off on this suggestion because I felt the situation was probably something that the embassy could handle better. But we were down to our last straw.

Pleskit looked startled at the suggestion, but then he bent his *sphen-gnut-ksher* in acknowledgment.

There was only one problem. When we called the police and explained the situation, the guy who answered the phone said, "Yeah, yeah, yeah. And my mother is from Mars. Leave me alone, kid. I got enough real problems to deal with. I don't need your prank phone calls."

"They think we're faking!" I cried angrily.

"Okay, we'll have to deal with this ourselves," said Pleskit. "Tim is always taking decisive action. It is time I learned to do the same thing."

"But what can we do?" I asked.

"We'll start by tracking the limo."

"That's impossible. It's long gone by now."

Pleskit smiled. "You are thinking in terms of Earth technology, Rafaella. Tracking the limo will be child's play for us. Literally. I have an old detective kit I got when I was much closer to the egg. It has several devices that should be of use to us."

Now he was starting to make me nervous. "You can't go out looking for the limo, Pleskit. You're just about the most recognizable person on the planet. If those anti-alien wackos catch you, there's no telling what they might do."

"I know that," said Pleskit. "Actually, I have thought

much about the problem of my traveling here since that time I ran away to keep the authorities from frying my Veeblax. I believe I have a solution. Wait here."

He scurried away. I began pacing nervously up and down the hall. Every minute we delayed, Ralph was getting farther away. What was he up to? More important, what was he going to do with the boys?

After what seemed like hours but was actually only about fifteen minutes, I felt a tug on the leg of my jeans. Looking down, I saw Ronald standing beside my sneaker, staring up at me.

I love hamsters — and hamsteroid mutants — so normally I would have been delighted to see him. But right then I was so stressed out that I didn't even bend down to pick him up, as I normally would have.

Ronald looked hurt. "Are you mad about something?" he asked.

Then I did bend down. "Of course I'm not mad, Ronald. At least, I'm not mad at you. But we've got big trouble. Ralph has just kidnapped Tim and Jordan, and —"

"Good grief!" interrupted Ronald, pointing behind me. "Who's that?"

I turned and stared in astonishment.

CHAPTER 13

[TIM]
A LITTLE CABIN
IN THE WOODS

When the stun ray hit me, I felt as if some-
one had pulled the plug on my brain. The last thing I
remember was the glow of purple light and then . . .
nothing!

The next thing I knew, I was in the limousine. At
least, I assumed I was in the limo — or, to be more pre-
cise, the limo's trunk. It was pitch black and I could
smell auto fumes. Also, I could tell we were moving,
even though the ride was amazingly smooth.

My shoulders hurt. When I tried to move my arms, I
realized that my hands were tied behind my back.

"Jordan?" I whispered.

Farewell to Earth

"It's about time you woke up," he said.

"How long have *you* been awake?"

"Longer than you," he replied, by which I guessed that he meant two or three minutes. It annoyed me that he had come out of the stun sooner than I had, but there's never been any question that he is stronger than me.

I like to think the reason I was out longer was that I have more brains that needed to recover.

"Every time I get tangled up with you and Pleskit, I end up having a near-death experience," he said bitterly.

"Beats homework," I said, trying to be cheerful.

He didn't answer.

I started trying to wriggle out of the ropes that held my hands tied, but they were too tight. Suddenly I felt something furry brush against my hand. My first thought was that it was a rat, and I screamed and lurched toward Jordan.

"What is wrong with you?" he snarled.

"Something just crawled over my hand," I said. "I think there's a rat in here with us."

Then I felt it crawling on my head!

I screamed and tried to shake it off. It grabbed my ear, and suddenly a tiny voice was saying, "Stop being so stupid! I'm no rat! If you'll hold still, I'll see if I can chew through the ropes holding your hands together."

The voice was familiar, but I could hardly believe it. "Doris?" I said.

"Doris!" cried Jordan in alarm. "What's she doing here?"

"I don't know," I said. "I'm not even sure it's her."

The small, furry creature, whoever it was, had scrambled down behind me. I could feel it working at my bonds. It took all my strength not to twitch, partly because it was tickling me, partly because having something crawling over your hands when they are tied behind you and you are lying in pitch darkness is an incredibly creepy feeling.

I could feel the bonds start to loosen. But before my unseen helper could finish the job, the limousine came to a halt.

A scurrying sound told me that Doris — if that's who it was, and it was hard to imagine why that evil little creature would have been helping me — was scrambling for cover.

Farewell to Earth

A moment later Ralph opened the trunk and hauled us out — first Jordan, then me. At first I thought we must be in a garage. But as I looked around, I realized that the entire front of the building had lifted up to let the limousine drive in. Looking past the opening, I saw that we were somewhere out in the woods.

I thought about running, of course, since only my hands were tied, and I had some hope that the bonds might be weak enough now that I could break them. But Ralph had the ray gun in his hand, and I figured I wouldn't get more than three feet before I was out cold again. Right now it was more important to stay alert.

Ralph touched a button on the wall. The front of the building lowered itself back into place. Ralph smiled but still didn't say anything, which was starting to feel really creepy.

He touched another button, and a panel slid open in the floor.

Ralph gestured to the hole.

I glanced at Jordan. He looked terrified — which is to say, he looked the way I felt.

Ralph repeated his gesture impatiently.

I walked forward. When I got to the edge of the opening, I saw a silvery stairwell stretching down into the darkness.

I stepped in.

Jordan followed me.

Ralph, still holding his ray gun, came last. Since he was behind me, I held my hands close together, trying to hide any signs that my binding had been tampered with.

As soon as we were all below floor level, the panel slid back into place, sealing us in. At the same time, the walls began to glow, a silvery-blue shine that made my skin look weird.

I continued down the steps, counting as I went.

At fifty the steps ended, and we entered a silvery-sided tunnel about ten feet high and five feet wide. Though the tunnel appeared to come to a dead end about fifteen feet ahead of us, just before I reached that spot, the wall slid up to reveal a large room.

Inside the room three beings sat at a table. One was facing us; two had their backs to us.

I gasped in dismay. I knew the alien facing us — knew all too well the scaly gray skin and the thick hair

Farewell to Earth

that writhed and hissed as if he had a head full of snakes. His name was Harr-giss, and he had been the first enemy Pleskit and I had defeated, way back at the beginning of the year.

Clearly Ralph's treachery was even worse than we had thought.

"Well, well," said Harr-giss with a chuckle. "It looks as if we have company, Urkding."

Though this was the first time I had seen the alien he was speaking to, I recognized the name, and it made me shudder. Several months earlier an alien named Skizzdor had almost captured Pleskit during the school science fair. Though we had caught Skizzdor, he'd had an accomplice named Urkding, who had escaped.

When Urkding turned to look at us, I saw that she had the same huge eyes and pebbly orange skin that we had found when we'd removed Skizzdor's mask. The only difference was that Urkding's head was vastly larger.

As terrifying as it was to see the two of them, things got even worse when the third being stood up and turned around.

She appeared to be a tall, good-looking Earth woman.

I had never seen her before.

Jordan, however, obviously had. He cried out a single word that both astonished and horrified me.

The word, spoken as a question, was, *"Mom?"*

CHAPTER 14

[PLESKIT]
TEMPORARY EARTHLING

Rafaella gazed at me with an expression of amazement. "How did you do that?" she asked at last.

I looked at her appraisingly. "Do you think it works?"

"Are you kidding?" she asked, her eyes still wide. "If I didn't know you, I'd swear you were an Earthling!"

"You mean he's not?" asked Ronald, who was standing next to her. He squinted up at me. "Who are you?"

"It's Pleskit," said Rafaella. She reached out and touched my pale face, then my brown hair. "Where's your *sphen-gnut-ksher*?"

I grimaced. "I had to strap it down, which was fairly

painful. Then I sprayed on a colorizing agent to give my skin this bizarre pink shade. Once that was done, I put on this wig, donned some standard Earthling clothing, and there you go — instant Earth kid!"

She walked around me, studying me carefully. Ronald followed, mimicking her motions.

"You look more human than some of the kids in our school," she said at last.

"Thanks . . . I think. At least I will be able to move around in the world without being detected. Come on, we have to get started. We can go out through the garage. After that we'll have to separate."

"Why?" asked Rafaella, sounding startled.

"Because it is vital that you meet the Fatherly One at the studio as planned so you can fill him in on what is happening."

"I don't know about leaving you alone out there, Pleskit," she said reluctantly.

"Rafaella, I have had a year to absorb your Earthly customs. I may not be perfect in my understanding of the planet, but I think I know enough to get by."

"Besides," said Ronald, "I'm going with him."

I looked at him skeptically.

Farewell to Earth

"I don't know what's going on," he said. "But you and your Fatherly One have been kind to me. If there's trouble, I want to help. Just because I'm little doesn't mean I can't be useful!"

"You don't have to tell me that," I said, remembering the incredible bravery he had showed when he'd carried the escape device into the Monster Dimension to save McNally. "Well then, you can come. But you'll have to stay hidden! No one will believe I'm an Earthling if I have an intelligent hamsteroid tagging along with me."

Rafaella took a deep breath. "Okay," she said. "I suppose you're right. But promise me you won't do anything crazy."

"I will be cautious," I said, raising my hand and making the belch of sincerity.

"As will I," said Ronald, making the same gesture but without the belch.

I scooped him up and put him in the pocket of my pants, which were stylishly baggy.

"All right," said Rafaella, still sounding reluctant. "Let's get going."

I hurried to my room to get the tracking device

I needed from my Junior Cosmic Detective Kit. I had almost thrown the kit away before we'd left for Earth because I thought it was sort of babyish. Now I was glad I hadn't.

Tracker in hand, I rejoined Rafaella, and we went down to the garage. I went to a back corner and pulled out a blue-and-silver capsule about four feet long.

"What's that?" asked Rafaella.

"It's my scootcar. I brought it from home, but I haven't had a chance to use it since I've been here."

She wrinkled her brow, an Earthling way of indicating puzzlement.

"Basically, it is an aerodynamic cartridge that rides on a pad of air. It is well cushioned inside, so the child who uses it will be protected against collisions at speeds up to —" I stopped and did a quick calculation to convert to Earth units. "Speeds up to one hundred seventy-five miles per hour."

"That thing can go one hundred seventy-five miles per hour?" asked Rafaella in astonishment.

"Faster, actually. But it's not so safe after that."

She shook her head, and we started up the ramp that leads to the surface. Before we opened the door

Farewell to Earth

to the outside, I used the tracking device to get a reading on the limo. The device flashed blue, indicating it had locked on to the trail.

"Be careful," said Rafaella yet again.

"Good luck at the studio," I replied. Then I climbed into the scootcar, which was floating about three inches above the ground. With a final wave to Rafaella, I shot away to begin my search for Tim and Jordan.

Once I was out of Thorncraft Park, I realized I had a problem—the kind of thing I hadn't thought about because, despite my somewhat boastful comment, I wasn't as familiar with Earth ways as I had thought.

The problem, of course, was where to drive the scootcar. It was too fast for the sidewalks, and I quickly realized that I was not really supposed to have something like this on the road.

Finally I got out and set the airpad on ultralow, so it looked as if I were dragging the scootcar. Holding the tracker in my left hand, keeping it pointed at the street, I followed the limo's trail.

After about fifteen minutes I came to the entrance ramp to a major highway. Clearly it was not a place for walking. So I mounted the tracker on the front of the scootcar, climbed back in, and shot up the ramp.

The looks on the faces of the other drivers as I passed them in my little scootcar would have been quite amusing had I not been so concerned about Tim and Jordan.

To make things worse, suddenly I heard a siren behind me. Glancing over my shoulder, I saw the flashing red lights of a police car.

Confusion seized me. It was possible that if the police stopped me, they would believe my story and follow me as I trailed the limo. But it seemed equally possible that they would just haul me off to jail and that I would end up not only losing my chance to save Tim and Jordan but disgracing the Fatherly One in the process.

I did the only thing I could think of: I jammed the scootcar into high. Instants later I was four feet above the roadway and traveling at nearly two hundred miles per hour.

Soon the police car was far behind me. Unfortunately, the driver must have radioed for help, because other police cars kept showing up as I passed more

Farewell to Earth

on-ramps. None of them could catch me, of course. Even so, I was glad I had spent so much time driving the scootcar when I was younger.

Ronald, who had climbed out of my pants pocket, was standing on the seat beside me, sometimes shouting, "Go, Pleskit, Go!" and other times putting his little paws over his eyes and crying, "We're gonna die! We're gonna die!"

In about ten minutes we were well away from the city, and the traffic had thinned to almost nothing.

I dropped the speed of the scootcar.

After another few miles the tracker showed me that the limo had left the highway.

Slowing down even more, we continued to follow the trail.

Soon we were on a small country road. Then an even smaller one. Then we turned onto a dirt road and then, to my surprise, onto something that was hardly a road at all, just a bumpy, rutted set of tracks that led into the woods.

The trail came to a dead stop at a little cabin.

"Where's the limo?" asked Ronald.

"I don't have the slightest idea," I said, feeling totally baffled.

Ronald climbed back into my pocket. I steered the scootcar to a clump of bushes where it would be hidden from sight. Then I got out and started toward the cabin door.

I was halfway there when someone grabbed me from behind and clamped a hand over my mouth.

CHAPTER 15

[JORDAN]
RELATIVITY

I know I'm not the only kid who's spent a lot of his life feeling as if he was different, as if he didn't quite fit in, as if there was something strange about him. Even Tim claims to have felt that way.

But standing there in that weird room, facing the gray-skinned alien with the snaky hair, the big-headed orange alien with the pebbly skin, and my mother, I suddenly knew, bone deep, that I was more of an outsider than I had ever imagined.

At first, I didn't really think Mom was an alien. Even when she glared at me and snarled, "What are you doing here, Jordan? You know that I have forbidden you to get involved in these matters!" I just figured that she was an Earthling who had somehow gotten mixed up in this plot. That alone was enough to make me feel as if I had been punched in the head.

But when Harr-giss, the gray-skinned alien, put his hand on Mom's shoulder and said, "I told you no good would come of marrying while you were in exile on this backward planet, Aila-kaspa," I suddenly felt so dizzy that I was afraid I would fall down.

"Aila-kaspa?" I repeated, barely able to get the word past my suddenly dry throat.

"That was my name on my home world," said Mom, heaving a sigh. "I did try to shield you from this, Jordan." She smiled slightly. "Or perhaps I should say 'Jour-dane,' as we would on Respail."

My cheeks were burning, and I could feel tears welling up in my eyes. "I don't understand—"

"Oh, don't be stupid," she snapped. "I didn't raise you to be an idiot. It's obvious that I am not originally from this misbegotten planet."

I was too shocked to do anything but babble. "But

Farewell to Earth

you don't look . . . Are you my real mo — Is that a mask? . . . How could —"

"Stop blithering!" she ordered. "Of course this is my real face. Fifteen planets in the galaxy are populated by the strain of life that gave rise to both the people of Respail and the people of Earth. Earth, of course, is the least developed of them — which is why Respail uses it as a prison planet."

"You're a prisoner here?" I asked in horror.

At the same time, Tim said, "You mean there are others here like you?"

Mom smiled, which is not always the most pleasant of sights. "Yes, I am a prisoner. And yes, Tim, there are others like me here — more than you can imagine!" Then, her eyes narrowing in that cold look I know so well, she added, "Of course, being a prisoner in a place like this gives one a lot of room for maneuvering, especially in times like these."

"Does Dad know about this?" I asked.

My mother and the other two aliens burst into laughter.

"Let's save the personal chatter for later," said

Urkding, the orange-skinned alien. "We have other matters to tend to."

"Untie the boy," said my mother to Ralph. "Jourdane, you can sit over there."

Ralph undid the ropes holding my hands together. I went to the chair my mother had indicated. I wanted to look at Tim, to see what he thought of all this, but didn't dare, because I was so —

To tell you the truth, I can't even name what I was feeling, it was such a weird stew of emotions. But I was afraid I was going to burst into tears at any second.

"All right," said my mother, turning to Ralph. "Do you have the Grand-bot ready to put in place?"

Ralph nodded.

"The Grand-bot?" asked Tim.

"A little replacement for your school principal," said Harr-giss.

"What are you planning to have him do?" I cried, suddenly worried about my friends.

"Oh, don't be absurd, Jour-dane," said my mother. "The point isn't to have him do anything bad. We just want to put the 'bot in place so we can unmask it.

Farewell to Earth

People will go crazy when they think an alien robot replaced a school principal."

"Between that and the Linnsy story, we expect to have Earthlings rioting in the streets demanding that Meenom leave," said the orange-skinned alien, twisting her fingers in her ears. "The Trading Federation is already on the verge of declaring his mission a failure. It's only going to take a bit more to get them to withdraw the franchise, and then our coalition can take over." She winked at me, a startling gesture coming from an alien. "You could end up a very rich young man, Jour-dane."

I didn't say anything. I didn't know what to say. I felt dizzy from all that was happening, all I was finding out. And I couldn't figure out where my loyalty should be. Was it with my mother, who had pretty much raised me but done it in a lie? Was it with my father, who wasn't around much but at least was a real Earthling? Was it with my planet? If I was only half Earthling, was this even really my planet?

"The information we have channeled to Mort Sludge has done its work," said Harr-giss. "Earth is at the boiling point, and it won't take much to push the planet over the edge into turmoil." He turned to Ralph. "Are you ready for your appointment?"

"I'm looking forward to it," he said.

I was startled by the sound of his voice. I knew I recognized it, but I couldn't figure out where I had heard it before.

"Good luck," said my mother. "It should be interesting." She waited until Ralph had left the room, then said, "And now I think it is time we dealt with Mr. Tompkins here."

"What do you have in mind, Aila?" asked Harr-giss. "I hope it's suitable, given the amount of trouble the boy has caused us over this last year."

"I believe it is time for my son to prove himself," said Mom. She pulled a ray gun from her belt, then said, "Drop a shield, Urkding!"

The orange alien went to the wall and pushed a button. Though you couldn't see it, I could sense a change in the room.

Mom put out her hand and made a rapping motion. She appeared to be simply hitting the air, but the hard sound made it clear something else was happening.

"Invisible barrier," she said. "I'm going to join Harr-

Farewell to Earth

giss and Urkding on the other side of it. I'll leave this ray gun here with you, Jour-dane."

The knot in my stomach was so hard, it hurt. "What for?" I asked.

She nodded toward Tim. "I think you understand me," she said, her face hard.

Then she walked to the edge of the room, placed the ray gun on the floor, and slipped around the barrier.

I stared at her in horror.

The three aliens looked back at me.

I turned to Tim.

He was looking at me with an expression I could not read.

I went to pick up the ray gun.

CHAPTER 16

[PLESKIT]
RESCUE MISSION

"Shhh!" hissed a voice in my ear. "Don't make a sound."

Still keeping one hand clamped over my mouth, my captor turned me slowly around.

My eyes widened in astonished relief. It was McNally!

He stared at me curiously for a moment, as if he didn't recognize me. Then I remembered that I now had pink skin and a full head of brown hair.

McNally squeezed his eyes shut, shook his head, then looked at me again, seemingly as astonished as I had been. "Pleskit, is that you?"

He was still whispering.

I nodded —the only way I could answer with his hand over my mouth.

"Shhh," he cautioned again as he removed his hand. He glanced around, then led me to a nearby tree. We stood on the far side of it, which gave us some shelter from the cottage.

"All right," he demanded. "What are you doing here? And what the heck happened to your skin?"

Keeping my voice low, I said, "Ralph kidnapped Tim and Jordan. I used a tracking device to follow the limo to this spot. But I can't figure out where it's gone."

"Oh, cripes," muttered McNally. "I'm glad I got here in time to stop you from going into that cabin by yourself."

"What are *you* doing here, anyway?" I asked.

"Some tracking of my own," said McNally. "After I was fired, I started working on this independently. I knew there was something fishy going on, and I had already started to suspect Ralph was involved with it. This morning I got a tip that led me here."

"A tip?" I asked.

He looked concerned. "It was a phone call from Doris."

"Yikes!" cried Ronald, sticking his head out of my pocket. "Turn back. Run away. It's a trap!"

Farewell to Earth

"Could be," said McNally grimly. "But I felt I had to check it out."

"But how could Doris make a phone call?" I asked. "She's a hamster!"

"Please," said Ronald. "We are intelligent hamsteroid beings. That's different."

"Sorry," I said. "Didn't mean to offend you, Ronald. But I still don't see how Doris could have made the call. How would she even get your number?"

"Well, she seems to make free run of the school after hours," said McNally. "My guess is that she went into Grand's office and got my home number from his Rolodex; I gave it to him after I was . . . released from duty. I wanted him to be able to contact me in case of an emergency. It would be no problem for Doris to push the speaker button on his phone and then punch in my number."

"And what did she say?" I asked.

"She gave me directions to this place and said that if I wanted to find the source of all the trouble, I should come here. She also warned me to be cautious — which is not something you normally do if you're trying to lure someone into a trap."

Suddenly we heard a noise. Pressing close to the tree, we peered around the edge of it—McNally on one side, me on the other.

The entire front wall of the cabin lifted up, revealing the embassy limousine. The car, which had seemed such a safe place to me for so long, now filled me with a sense of fear.

It rolled out of the cabin. Immediately the wall lowered back into position.

"Should we follow it?" I whispered as the limo drove past our tree.

McNally shook his head. "We can trail it later if we have to. My guess is that Ralph dumped Tim and Jordan somewhere inside the cabin — he wouldn't want to be driving around with them in the limo any more than he had to. Too dangerous. I'm going to go up and scout the place out. You stay here."

"I'm going with you," I said.

"I said to stay here!" repeated McNally, sounding angry.

"You are not my bodyguard now," I replied stubbornly. "We are in this together."

He closed his eyes for a second, then said, "I want

you to stay here for tactical reasons. That way, if something happens to me, you can still escape and get the word out. If I'm not back in ten minutes, get into that scootcar and go for help."

It was hard to argue with this, and I watched sullenly as McNally approached the cabin. But the door wouldn't open — possibly it wasn't really a door at all, since the cabin was designed as a hiding place for the limousine.

McNally tugged on it several times, then tried the window to its right. That would not open either. He was just turning to come back to me when the front wall of the cabin lifted again. He raced to the side of the cabin, to hide himself, but the space inside seemed to be deserted.

He came cautiously back around the corner.

I decided to join him.

We stepped inside.

"Glad you could make it," said a tiny voice. "I've been waiting for you."

CHAPTER 17

[JORDAN]
THE OTHER PRISONER

The ray gun—shiny, purple, cold—was trembling in my hand.

I knew what my mother wanted me to do. But that was about the only thing in the world I knew right then, since everything else I'd thought I knew, everything I had been told since I had been born, had been stripped away from me.

My mother was an alien. Which meant that I was half alien. I looked around, hoping some hole would open up and swallow me.

"Go on, Jour-dane," said my mother. Her voice was starting to sound harsh, ragged.

Farewell to Earth

I recognized that tone, and I didn't like it.

Still I hesitated.

"I didn't raise you to be a fool, Jour-dane!" she snapped. "Do what you need to do to prove yourself!"

She was serious.

So I did the only thing I could think of.

I pointed the ray gun at myself.

"Jordan!" cried Tim. "Don't!"

At the same moment, my mother came racing out from behind the barrier and grabbed my hand. "You little idiot!" she hissed.

She tried to pull the ray gun away from me, but I wouldn't let her. We began to fight for it. She hooked her foot behind my knee and pushed on my chest. I fell backward, with her on top of me. "I didn't raise you for this," she said as she wrenched the ray gun from my hand. She stood up and pointed it at me.

"Go ahead and shoot," I said, trying not to sob.

She rolled her eyes in disgust and made an adjustment on the ray gun. She pulled the trigger. A crimson ray shot out. I slumped back, unable to move but still totally alert.

"My apologies for the behavior of my son, Harr-giss,"

she said. "He's experiencing some emotional instability due to shock. Urkding, help me put him in with the other prisoner."

I assumed she meant Tim.

I was wrong. Mom and Urkding picked me up, Mom holding my shoulders, Urkding my feet, and carried me to the back of the room. A door opened — I couldn't see how she did it — and they tossed me in.

The door closed, plunging the room into darkness.

But in the brief instant of light, I saw who the other prisoner was.

I was too numb to feel anything. But even if I had been able to summon up a new emotion, I don't know if it would have been hope, horror, or despair.

CHAPTER 18

[PLESKIT]
UNEXPECTED ALLY

"Doris!" I cried. "What are you doing here?" I bent to look at her more closely. "And what happened to you?"

The little mutant was no longer the proud, sneering hamsteroid who had treated Tim, Jordan, and me with such contempt the night she shrank us and forced us to don hamster suits. Her face had less of the fierce intelligence; her body was less like that of a two-legged being and more like that of a . . . well, of a hamster.

Her orange uniform was tattered and dusty, and it was clear that it was hard for her to hold her tiny ray gun.

"I'm reverting," she said bitterly.

"Oh, I knew you should have abandoned your career of evil and come to the embassy with me," said Ronald, who was peering over the edge of my pocket.

"Shut up, Ronald," said Doris wearily. She looked up at us. "I owe you an apology, Pleskit," she said. "You too, McNally. Back when I was just a hamster, they called me Doris the Delightful. Wiktor's mutating ray twisted something inside me, made me into something that wasn't truly me."

Suddenly that twist showed in her eyes, a flash of rage that I found momentarily terrifying. "He promised he would come back for me!" she shrieked, shaking her tiny fist at the sky. "He promised . . . all sorts of things." She plucked at her filthy uniform. "This isn't me," she said, her voice trembling. "I was born a hamster. All I want now is to die a hamster." Suddenly her voice turned hard again. "That, and my revenge. That's why I contacted you, McNally. That's why I opened the door for you just now. This group is connected with Wiktor, and I want them to pay for what he did to me! I want them to pay *big!*"

It was hard to tell if Doris was sincere, faking to draw us into a trap, or just plain losing her small, hamstery mind.

Farewell to Earth

I heard a tiny sound from my pocket and realized that Ronald was weeping. I remembered that we had suspected he was in love with Doris, back when they shared a cage.

"All right, what's the situation here?" said McNally, squatting so he could look Doris in the face.

"The real action is underground. This cabin is just a disguise for the entrance to their headquarters."

"Are Tim and Jordan down there?" I asked eagerly.

"I expect so."

"Are they all right?"

"I don't know. I was in the trunk with them for a while."

"How did that happen?" asked McNally suspiciously.

"I gnawed a hole in the bottom of the trunk so I could get in and out of the thing whenever I wanted," she said. "I've been using it as a way to get back and forth from the city. I just happened to be in there when Ralph kidnapped them. I started to chew through Tim's bonds but got interrupted before I could finish. I would have sneaked down to check on them after Ralph took them out of the trunk, but I needed to stay up here to wait for McNally. I didn't expect to see you too, Pleskit.

What happened to your skin, anyway? Don't tell me you're mutating too."

"It's just a disguise," I said.

"Things are changing everywhere," said McNally. "What can you tell me about the enemy, Doris?"

"There are three of them, all aliens. One is called Urkding. Another, who looks astonishingly human, is named Aila-kaspa. The third is called Harr-giss."

"Harr-giss!" I cried in horror. "Oh, this is bad."

McNally nodded grimly, then said, "What about the layout of the place?"

Doris reached into her tattered uniform and pulled out several pieces of yellow paper. I recognized them as the kind of sticky notes Mr. Grand liked to use and wondered if she had stolen them from his desk.

"Here are some diagrams I made," she said, passing the papers to McNally. "Front way in, back entrance, rooms, all that kind of thing."

"How did you do all this?" I asked.

"Being small has its advantages," she said. "Being small, sneaky, and furious has even more."

McNally sat down and squinted at the diagrams.

Farewell to Earth

He was obviously having trouble reading them because they were so tiny.

"I've got something that can help," I said. I hurried back to where I had hidden the scootcar and pulled off the tracking device, which I carried back to McNally. "This has a magnifier in it," I said, showing him how to work it.

McNally got down on his hands and knees, spread the papers on the floor, and began to examine them through the tracking device.

"Okay," he said after a minute. "I think I see what we should do."

"We?" I asked hopefully.

"Yes, we," he said, sounding somewhat distressed. "I'll probably get in trouble for dragging you into this, but there's no time to go get help—the boys could be gone before we get back."

"You're not dragging me," I said. "I would fight to be allowed to come! I would follow you even if you forbade me! Besides . . . I'm still in disguise. You can always say you didn't know it was me!"

McNally laughed and shook his head. "That would be even worse! I'd be a heck of a bodyguard if I didn't know my own client just because he changed his skin color. On the other hand, using that disguise is what I've got in mind."

"What do you mean?" asked Ronald.

McNally looked around uneasily. "Let's get out of here," he said. "We don't want them to catch us while we're working this out."

A few minutes later we were standing beside the scootcar. McNally stuck the notes with Doris's diagrams all over the front of it. Then he squatted beside them and began to explain his plan.

Fifteen minutes later I raced up to the cabin and let out a bloodcurdling scream. "Help!" I cried, pounding on the front door. "Please, someone, help me!"

My face was stained with mud. My clothes were torn, as if I had been racing through brambles.

"They're coming!" I screamed. "They're coming for me! Help! Helllllp meeeeee!"

It took a few minutes of this, but pretty soon a tall, good-looking Earth woman flung open the door and grabbed me by the arm. She did not ask what was wrong. She did not offer to help me. She just dragged me inside and hissed, "For heaven's sake, shut up!"

Farewell to Earth

"I can't!" I cried. "Terrible aliens are trying to get me. Please hide me! Please!"

The woman stared at me as if I had lost my mind.

From a speaker on the wall behind her a voice said, "What's going on up there?"

"Something crazy," said the woman.

"Aliens!" I cried. "Aliens trying to abduct me!"

"Shut up!" snarled the woman, giving me a shake. Then she pulled out a ray gun and pointed it at me.

Immediately I put my hands above my head. "Don't shoot!" I cried. "Don't shoot!"

She shot.

I crumpled to the floor and closed my eyes.

A few minutes later I felt two sets of hands pick me up. I lay limp and unmoving as they carried me down a long set of stairs, then dumped me onto a floor.

"Who is that?" asked a voice that I recognized as belonging to Harr-giss.

"I don't know," said the woman who had met me at the door.

Everything was going exactly as we had planned. I was inside their hideout. They had not recognized me. I had properly shielded myself against the stun ray. And

127

my pretended collapse seemed to have fooled them.

I remained on the floor, making no visible movement yet carefully readying myself to unleash the survival tactic every Hevi-Hevian child is taught at an early age. It is a tactic that we hope never to have to use. But these were extraordinary circumstances.

Actually, I had been preparing for this moment from well before I entered the cabin. Now, as I lay on the floor of the conspirators' hideout, I continued to suck in air. Finally I thought I was ready.

I tensed my stomach, hardened it, waited until they had turned away from me.

Then I released the most horrible personal weapon known to any Hevi-Hevian: the dreaded Fart of Doom!

CHAPTER 19

[TIM]
THE BATTLE BEGINS

When some kind of fuss started in the cabin above us, Harr-giss sent Aila-kaspa up to check on it.

A few minutes later, Urkding went up to join her.

And a few minutes after that, the two of them returned, dragging what looked like an ordinary Earth kid with them. They dumped him onto the floor.

My questions about what was going on were answered a moment later when the kid's seemingly lifeless body emitted an incredible "SPLOOORCH!"

The sound, which echoed off the walls, was followed by the most horrifying odor I have ever smelled. Imagine bad perfume, an angry skunk, rotten sauerkraut, and a backed-up sewer all combined, and you'll be halfway there. Eyes watering, I dropped to the floor, coughing, gagging, and gasping for breath.

So did Harr-giss, Urkding, and Aila-kaspa.

At the same instant, the kid sprang to his feet. "Now, McNally!" he shouted. *"Now!"*

A microsecond later, McNally burst into the room, coming through the same door where they had taken Jordan not long before. He had his gun in one hand. With his other he was holding a handkerchief over his mouth and nose.

"Don't anyone move!" he shouted.

For an instant I thought it was all over.

Then Jordan's mother did something that astonished me. Lifting herself up from the floor, she opened her mouth and shot out a tongue that had to be four feet long. It wrapped around McNally's ankle and yanked him off balance. His feet went up, and he went down, hitting the floor hard. The gun fell out of his hand.

It was time to move. I wrenched my arms apart, tearing open the bonds that Doris had weakened back when we'd been in the trunk.

Harr-giss, still coughing and gasping, began to

crawl toward the gun. I did the same thing. It was hard to see because my eyes were still watering from that phenomenal fart. Even so, I got to the weapon just ahead of him. But as I stretched my hand toward it, Harr-giss clamped his hand over my arm. I squirmed around and gave the gun a solid kick that sent it sliding across the floor.

Harr-giss's snakelike hair writhed in fury. He flung himself onto me. I was afraid he was going to strangle me. But suddenly I heard a tiny voice cry, "Leave him be!"

It was Ronald. The little hamsteroid leaped atop Harr-giss's head and began biting and pulling the writhing strands of hair. Harr-giss howled in agony and rolled over, almost smashing Ronald, who leaped aside just in time.

I staggered to my feet, still choking on the pungent air. Urkding lunged at me. My Koo Muk Dwan training took over. *"Hee-yuk Fwah!"* I cried, ducking underneath her. Then I leaped up with the move called "the Sun Also Rises" just in time to strike her in the stomach.

"All right!" shouted a sharp voice. "That's just about enough. Freeze where you are, or the hamster dies!"

I looked to my right. Harr-giss was holding Ronald

Farewell to Earth

above his head. It was clear that he was ready to fling the little mutant against the wall with all his strength if we didn't surrender at once.

I put up my hands.

So did McNally.

So did Pleskit.

Aila-kaspa grabbed one of the ray guns. Urkding got another.

Harr-giss began to laugh. "You sentimental fools," he said. "Willing to give yourselves up for the sake of a mere — aiiieee!"

Dropping Ronald, who landed on the desk, he grabbed for his ankle. No sooner had he touched it than he straightened up again, howling with pain and anger.

A writhing mass of fur was clamped on to his hand.

"Doris!" cried Ronald, pushing himself to his feet. "Let go! Let go!"

Urkding moved to help Harr-giss.

I sprinted forward to stop her.

Aila-kaspa spun toward me and fired.

CHAPTER 20

[JORDAN]
THE BATTLE ENDS

When McNally came through the place where Mom and Urkding had dumped me, I was still in the grip of the stun ray. When I heard the battle break out in the other room, I tried to get up so that I could join in, but I fell down twice before I made it to my feet. My entire body had that pins-and-needles feeling you get when your foot goes to sleep.

When I finally got to the door, I saw a terrible scene.

Urkding and my mother, facing away from me, had ray guns in their hands. Tim, McNally, and some Earth kid I had never seen before had their hands in the air. Ronald was standing on the desk, pleading and weep-

Farewell to Earth

ing. Harr-giss was struggling with something attached to his hand. Suddenly Urkding started forward. An instant later, so did Tim. Mom spun toward him. I could tell she was going to zap him with the ray gun.

Stumbling forward, I grabbed her around the waist and pulled her to the floor. The ray gun fired, but the beam of crimson light went astray.

Mom turned on me with a howl of fury.

Let me tell you this: a kid shouldn't have to get into a fistfight with his own mother.

But then, a kid's mother shouldn't lie to him about what planet she was born on. A kid's mother shouldn't plot to take over the world without even telling him what's going on.

While we were struggling, I heard a battle raging around me. I had to ignore it.

I'm strong, and I'm big for my age.

Mom is strong too. Even so, I had the advantage for a moment, since I had taken her by surprise. I was holding her by the shoulders, forcing them to the floor, which put us face-to-face.

"Jour-dane," she whispered. "How can you do this? I'm your mother!"

"You're a liar," I hissed back — even now, in the middle of this insane battle, wanting to keep this private. "You've lied to me all my life!"

"I was just waiting for the right time," she said. "And look what we've almost got in our hands — the chance to control more money than you've ever dreamed of!"

"How do I know you're not lying now?" I sobbed.

"How did I raise such a sentimental fool?" she answered, arching her back and flipping us over so that now I was pinned to the floor.

I struggled to break free but couldn't. Was she too strong for me . . . or was it that I didn't have the heart to fight her?

It didn't matter, because as quickly as it had started, it was over. I had distracted her long enough that Tim and McNally had been able to subdue Harr-giss and Urkding, and now they were trying to pull my mother off me. She shrieked with rage.

Suddenly her tongue lashed out. I almost threw up when I saw it stretch to a sickening length. It wrapped around McNally's neck, and I saw the muscles in her own neck bulge as she tried to choke him with it.

At that moment the kid I hadn't recognized, the

Farewell to Earth

one I had thought was an Earthling, pulled off his wig to reveal a bald, purple head.

"That's about enough of that!" he cried, pulling up his *sphen-gnut-ksher*.

Then, just as he had done to me the first day we met, Pleskit released a bolt of energy.

My mother sighed and collapsed to the floor.

CHAPTER 21

[TIM]
AFTER THE BATTLE

At one time, seeing Pleskit zap Jordan's mom would have been the highlight of my day.

Now it just made me sad.

But there was more sorrow to come. As we surveyed the room, checking to make sure that Harr-giss, Urkding, and Aila-kaspa were all safely subdued, I became aware of a small, heartbreaking sound.

It was coming from the desk.

I hurried over.

Ronald was kneeling there, clutching Doris in his tiny arms. Her breathing was ragged, her eyes dim.

"Don't go, Doris," whispered Ronald. "Please don't leave me."

Farewell to Earth

Doris reached up and stroked his face with a tiny paw, more hamster-like now than it had been the last time I'd seen her.

"Dear Ronald," she said. "Please forgive me. I was terribly mean to you the last time we were together. But that wasn't the real me. It wasn't." She paused, then murmured, "You're a good hamster, Ronald."

"And you're delightful, Doris," he whispered.

Doris twitched. Her head fell back. Then her eyes closed, and she breathed no more.

A terrible silence fell over the room, broken only by Ronald's soft weeping. Pleskit, Jordan, McNally, and I stood looking down at the two hamsters, one with a broken body, the other with a broken heart, and did not know what to say. I brushed away a tear that was trickling down my cheek.

Then we heard another sound — a groan from the room where Jordan's mother had stashed him after he'd been zapped.

Jordan's eyes widened. "I almost forgot! Have I got a surprise for you. Come here."

I followed him to the door.

When I looked inside, I began to cry again — this time from sheer happiness.

CHAPTER 22

[RAFAELLA]
MEET MORT SLUDGE

When the aliens had first announced that they were going to put their embassy in Syracuse, the major news services had scrambled to throw together a temporary studio for all the broadcasting they knew they would be doing from here. They've been working on the place ever since, and it's pretty well set up now.

That studio was where I was supposed to connect with Meenom for his showdown broadcast with Mort Sludge.

As soon as Pleskit and I separated, I rode my bike back to my house and got cleaned up a little. Then I begged Uncle Alonso to drive me to the studio. He grumbled about it but finally agreed. I could tell that he was torn between being appalled that I was going to speak on behalf of the aliens and being excited about the chance to meet Mort Sludge, who he considered a great hero and patriot.

The studio had been alerted that I was going to appear with the ambassador, so we had no problem getting in. They sent us to a place they call the green room, which is where people wait before they go on the air. While Uncle Alonso filled up on coffee and doughnuts, I paced around waiting for Meenom. I felt a huge wave of relief the instant he walked in. I started to hurry over to him, but, to my horror, Uncle Alonso got there first.

I figured he was going to start some anti-alien rant, and I was getting my apologies ready when Uncle Alonso astonished me by gushing, "Mr. Ambassador, I'm Rafaella's uncle, and I am *so* pleased to meet you!"

It took me a minute to figure out what was going on: Uncle Alonso was starstruck!

In another situation I would have found it funny to watch him suck up to Meenom after all the time I had spent listening to his anti-alien ranting. But right now we didn't have time for that. Touching Meenom on the arm, I said, "We need to discuss our strategy before we go on the air, Mr. Ambassador. In private." I tried to show with my eyes that it was urgent.

He must have gotten the message, because he asked Uncle Alonso to excuse us, then took me aside.

Quickly I told him everything that had happened that afternoon.

He looked shaken, sick even, and for a minute I feared he might slip into that dazed state that Pleskit calls *kleptra*. This scared me all the more. I want adults to be strong and confident in an emergency. But Meenom quickly pulled himself together. Taking a comm-device from the pocket of his robe, he put out a distress call. I was impressed with how calm he was able to make his voice sound when he said, "Mr. President, this is Meenom Ventrah. I need your help."

Soon he had the entire United States government working on the situation.

"All right," he said when that was done. "Let's go get ready for that interview."

"You mean you're not going to cancel it?" I asked in surprise.

"Certainly not! Backing out now would only make

things worse. There is nothing I can do personally to help Pleskit, Tim, or Jordan at this moment. What I *can* do is continue trying to help the people of Earth. If I cannot calm this situation, the Helmscott Faction may be able to take over the franchise. That would be a disaster for your planet. I will do all in my power to prevent it."

I looked at him with new admiration.

Five minutes before it was time to go on the air, Mort Sludge came in to meet us. "So pleased that you could make it, Ambassador," he said cordially, shaking Meenom's hand.

I was amazed. Could this be the same guy who had been spewing such vicious anti-alien propaganda over the Internet and on the radio?

Once we were actually on the air, it became clear that it was. Sludge turned out to be a real two-faced skeeze, a weaselly whiner who had acted nice enough when it was just the three of us in the green room but who shouted and interrupted and made misstatements of facts as soon as we were on the air.

The studio audience, about a hundred and fifty

people invited especially for the occasion, seemed to be loving it. Personally, it made me embarrassed to be an Earthling.

Sludge was even worse when it was my turn. "Aren't you worried about being abducted too?" he asked.

"I feel completely safe with Pleskit," I replied. "He's been a very good friend."

"And it doesn't make you nervous to visit him at the embassy?" asked Sludge.

I looked at him as if he were crazy. "Why should it?"

"Are you sure they haven't used some alien mind control device on you?" he asked, as if he were talking to a kindergartner.

"Of course not!" I said indignantly.

A sneer twisted Sludge's face. Turning to the audience, he said, "And what else *would* she say if she were under the aliens' control? Of course she denies it!"

It was the most infuriating thing I had ever heard. The more I denied it, the more Sludge said that proved it.

Clearly not willing to believe — or admit — that I might be telling the truth, he turned his attention back to Meenom. I got the feeling he wanted the audience to suspect that I wasn't even a real Earthling — maybe just some android that Meenom had manufactured for public relations purposes.

"All right, Ambassador," Sludge said, leaning close. "It's time to get to the real reason why we're here. I'm going to ask you the question that all of Earth wants answered: *Where is Linnsy Vanderhof?*"

"We have not spoken about this in order to respect the privacy of the family involved," Meenom began. "But since you have raised such an uproar about it, I can tell you that Linnsy was taken from Earth —"

"Aha! You admit it!" cried Sludge. Turning to the audience, he said, "You heard it from the ambassador himself. Linnsy Vanderhof was abducted from Earth by aliens!"

"That is not what I said!" objected Meenom.

But Sludge had shifted tactics. "Is it true that you have an enormous financial stake in what happens with your mission here on Earth?"

Meenom looked surprised and a little worried. "That is true," he said solemnly.

"Again he admits it!" cried Sludge. "So it must also be true that you have a financial stake in keeping the true fate of that poor girl secret. In the name of all Earthlings, I ask you again: *Where is Linnsy Vanderhof?*"

CHAPTER 23

[TIM]
THE RETURN

Lying on the floor, bound with some elec-
tronic thing that kept them in an unmoving state, was
Linnsy *vec* Bur.

"How do we set them free?" I cried, wiping aside
my tears.

"I know how to handle this," said Pleskit.

I still had not gotten used to him having disguised
himself as an Earthling—a disguise that looked even
weirder now that he had taken off his wig so that his bald,
purple head with its *sphen-gnut-ksher* was showing.

He knelt beside Linnsy *vec* Bur and made an adjustment to the blue ring that had been put around the waist

of the Linnsy part. I heard a slight fizzing sound, and all of a sudden their body, which had been rigid, relaxed.

"Thank you," they said, speaking in both their voices at the same time. They sat up and stretched. "It was truly distressing to be trapped that way while you four were fighting the enemy."

"How long have you been here?" I asked.

"A little over a week ago, we got a message from a friend of yours named Beebo that there was big trouble brewing around Linnsy's disappearance. We decided that the best way to solve the problem was to show up ourselves. But we were caught by the Helmscott Faction just outside your solar system and imprisoned here. We hope it is not too late for us to help out."

"Ohmigosh, the broadcast!" I cried. "You may still be able to help. What time is it, McNally?"

I asked McNally because I knew he always wore a watch. I used to try to, but I gave up because I always lost them.

He glanced at his wrist. "Ten minutes to three."

"Let's see if we can get them to the studio."

"What broadcast are you talking about?" asked Linnsy *vec* Bur.

"The Fatherly One is going to be debating an anti-alien jerk named Mort Sludge who has been making a big fuss about you — about the Linnsy part of you — being missing," said Pleskit.

The Linnsy portion began to laugh.

"What's so funny?" I asked.

"Mort Sludge," they said. "Have we got a surprise for him!"

"What is it?" asked Pleskit.

Both Linnsy and Bur smiled, which creates a somewhat weird effect. "Wait and see," they said. "We think you'll be amused."

While McNally got his car, which he had hidden in the brush about halfway along the rutted trail that led to the cabin, Linnsy *vec* Bur and Pleskit used the binding devices on Harr-giss, Aila-kaspa, and Urkding.

"Do you think they'll be all right here?" I asked.

"Should be," said Linnsy *vec* Bur. "As far as we know, there aren't any other members of their group on Earth."

"I'll have someone come out to pick them up as soon as we get to the studio," said McNally, who had come back into the room. He looked at Jordan. "You all right, son?" he asked gently.

Farewell to Earth

Jordan shook his head. "Not really," he said in a voice so soft that you could scarcely hear it.

"Don't blame you," said McNally. "I'd be pretty shook up too."

He went to the desk, where Ronald still crouched beside Doris's body, weeping softly. McNally murmured something I couldn't hear, then took out his handkerchief. Working gently, he wrapped it around Doris.

"Thank you," sniffed Ronald, putting his tiny hand on McNally's. Then he climbed into Pleskit's pocket.

We all piled into the car and headed for the studio.

Pleskit put his wig back on as we traveled. I was just as glad. He looked awfully weird as a half human, half alien.

Then I realized that that was exactly what Jordan really was. Except for the fact that his mother was a villain, I thought it was kind of cool.

I got the feeling Jordan didn't agree.

I was smart enough to keep my mouth shut.

We had no problem getting into the studio where Meenom and Sludge were having their showdown. As we came through the door, Sludge was saying, "In the name of all Earthlings, I ask you again: *Where is Linnsy Vanderhof?*"

"We can answer that question," said Linnsy *vec* Bur, speaking only in Linnsy's voice, which was clear and strong.

As one, the audience turned to see who was speaking. About half of them screamed. Two or three people fainted.

Linnsy *vec* Bur started toward the stage, where Mort Sludge was gaping as if he had just seen a ghost.

Meenom stood to greet them. "Thank you for coming back," he said. "Your timing is perfect."

"We're glad to be of service, old friend," said Linnsy *vec* Bur as they stepped onto the stage.

It was weird to hear them speak of Meenom as an old friend, but of course the ambassador *was* an old friend of Bur's. And whatever Bur knew and had experienced was part of Linnsy's life now too.

I looked at Jordan. He nodded. We moved to the side of the studio and began making our way toward the stage, as we had worked out in the car.

Linnsy *vec* Bur — half my old friend, half Meenom's old friend — turned to the cameras. Voices solemn, they said, "We understand that there has been a great deal of concern about the fate of the Linnsy half of us."

Farewell to Earth

"The poor girl has no mind of her own!" cried Sludge. "She's possessed by that alien!"

"Someone here is a tool of an alien conspiracy," replied Linnsy *vec* Bur. "But it is not us."

"What are you talking about?" demanded Sludge. He sounded belligerent, but you could see the fear in his eyes.

Jordan and I had made it to the edge of the stage. Linnsy *vec* Bur made a gesture. Jordan and I sprang forward and grabbed Sludge's arms, pinning him to his seat. He began to thrash and shout, crying out for help. People leaped up from their seats, ready to storm the stage.

"Wait just a moment, and you will see the truth!" cried Linnsy *vec* Bur.

They walked over to where we were holding Sludge. As they bent to loosen his collar, Linnsy winked at me.

Sludge whimpered. Linnsy *vec* Bur reached inside the collar. "Got it," they said, speaking in a single voice.

Then they peeled off Sludge's face.

I expected to see some hideous alien.

What I saw was even more shocking.

It was Ralph-the-Driver!

Farewell to Earth

"You traitor!" cried Meenom, sounding hurt and shocked.

"'Traitor' is right," said Linnsy *vec* Bur. They turned and looked directly into the cameras. "This man, who calls himself Mort Sludge, has been working for the alien embassy since it was established last September. How did he get into a position that required such high clearance? The answer is simple: he was *also* working for a rival alien group that was trying to sabotage the ambassador's mission — a group that was conspiring to take over the trading franchise with Earth so they could suck the planet dry."

"Prove it!" cried someone.

Linnsy *vec* Bur nodded toward the back of the studio. The door opened. McNally and two security guards he had summoned marched in Urkding and Harr-giss.

We had agreed, for Jordan's sake, to keep Aila-kaspa out of this part of things.

"These are the aliens Sludge was working for," said Linnsy *vec* Bur. "Surely those of you who follow these things will recognize Harr-giss, since he was unmasked in this very studio shortly after Ambassador Meenom's arrival."

Now the audience was really angry. "Traitor!" they

153

cried, pointing at Ralph, or Sludge, or whatever his name was. "Traitor!"

With a sudden squirm he wrenched himself free of the chair where Jordan and I had been holding him and lunged toward Linnsy *vec* Bur.

"Stop him!" I cried.

Pleskit yanked off his wig and, with a bolt of energy from his *sphen-gnut-ksher*, knocked Ralph into *kling-kphut*.

Ralph fell to the floor in a dreamy stupor. Pleskit staggered and dropped to his knees, drained by the energy release.

Meenom stared at his childling in astonishment.

At that moment we were interrupted again, this time by the arrival of Barvgis and Sookutan Krimble.

More gasps from the audience, who were getting more aliens than they had bargained for.

"Oh, stop it," I said sharply. "These are two of the nicest beings I have ever met."

Barvgis whispered something to Meenom.

The ambassador smiled and said, "Now *I* have an announcement to make — one that will affect the future of the entire planet."

CHAPTER 24

[PLESKIT]
THE INVITATION

The Fatherly One looked at the studio audience and then directly into the cameras that were transmitting his words all around the world.

"I have just accepted an offer to lease the Earth franchise, and its related *urpelli*, to an ethical coalition that will manage it for me. This coalition will be headed by my good friend Sookutan Krimble."

He gestured to *Frek* Krimble, who came up to stand beside him. Putting a hand on the *Frek*'s shoulder, the Fatherly One said, "I can tell you that this being has fought for your best interests from the first day that the Interplanetary Trading Federation agreed it was time to make contact with Earth. The group *yeeble* leads has your well-being at heart and will do their best to protect your planet from the difficult transitions that await you."

He paused, and I could tell that he was filled with emotion.

"My friends, it is hard for me to say what this will mean for Earth. I have been struggling for the last year to protect your planet from the kind of colonization and opportunism that your own so-called advanced countries have practiced on their less technological neighbors — the kind of strip-and-burn practices that would have sucked the wealth from your world and given it to people who would have become your oppressors.

"For a variety of reasons — including the treachery of 'Mort Sludge' — I was losing that battle. However, the tide has now turned. With the help of Sookutan Krimble, I have been able to have your planet established as a protectorate."

I heard some grumbling sounds from the audience. The Fatherly One raised his hands.

"If this sounds high-handed and makes you angry, you need only look to your own recent history to understand that in the eyes of the civilized galaxy, your current level of development makes you appear brutal and untamed. Try to imagine how easy it is for beings on peaceful, well-managed planets, when reading of your wars and your wanton devastation of your ecology, to think of you as unruly children who need a stabilizing hand. Or, worse, as war-stricken savages who deserve no consideration at all — a flawed species in the process of destroying itself.

"But I wish to offer, instead, a helping hand. The licensing of Gurp Two is going to generate an enormous amount of money. Had I maintained my hold on the franchise, my family unit would have become the richest in the galaxy.

"But how much money does one really need? One trades one's time and energy to gain it, and that is fair. But how much time? How much energy?"

He turned and extended a hand to me. I went to stand beside him. Putting his arm around me, he spoke to me instead of to the camera. "Enough is enough, my childling," he said.

I moved closer. Something was changing. My Fatherly One was returning to me.

He shifted to face the cameras again.

"It seems clear that the time is not right for Earth and the rest of the galaxy to interact on a fully established basis. So we are going to withdraw for the time being and leave you to follow your own destiny.

"However, we have a gift for you. Fifty percent of the income generated by the *urpelli* license will be deposited into a trust fund to be administered by all nations for the good of the planet.

"The wealth will be almost incalculable. And it leaves you facing a fantastic choice, my dear Earthlings: How will you spend this treasure? What choices will you make with this windfall?

"I beg you to remember this: every dollar you spend is an ethical decision. This is as true for individuals as it is for nations. So what will be your priorities?

"Will you feed the poor — or build new weapons?

"Will you fund the research that could end disease? Seek for ways to harness the full potential of your incredible minds? Solve the problem of interstellar travel?

"Or will all this only serve to make the rich grow richer?

"With this vast new treasure you can cleanse your planet of pollution, eradicate hunger, and educate all the children of all the nations."

He paused and smiled sadly. "Of course, the tragedy of your species is that you could be doing that already if you really wanted to. But this will make it a

Farewell to Earth

little easier — *if* that's what you decide to do."

He turned and motioned to Tim, Rafaella, and Jordan.

"Would you join me, please?"

Looking puzzled, they stepped up beside us.

We all listened in astonishment as the Fatherly One made his next statement.

"Though my family and I are leaving, I do not want to sever the lines of communication between Earth and Hevi-Hevi. To keep our peoples connected, it is my intention to invite Pleskit's entire sixth-grade class, along with their families, to spend the next year as my personal guests on Hevi-Hevi. This will be made possible by the payments generated from the licensing of Gurp Two.

"It is my deepest hope that this will be the beginning of a great friendship between our planets.

"We have much to offer you, my friends. But I think there are things we can learn as well — lessons about spontaneity, and courage, and the readiness to take action when it is necessary. Lessons of the sort I have learned from my young friends here, who have done more for Earth than you will ever realize."

He extended his hands, palms up, toward the cameras.

"May this be the beginning of a great friendship between our peoples."

CHAPTER 25

[TIM]
FAREWELL TO EARTH

(TRANSCRIPTION OF A RECORDING)

Okay, I'm dictating this into one of the little recorder devices we've all been given to take down our impressions of the next year. Hope this thing works!

I am standing with the class — well, most of the class. Misty Longacres and Brad Kent aren't with us, since their parents didn't want them to go. But the rest of us — Ms. Weintraub, the other kids, their parents, their brothers and sisters, even a couple of grandparents and Rafaella's uncle Alonso — are all standing here at the edge of an open meadow about three miles out of town, where the biggest field trip in history is about to start. McNally is with us too; Pleskit won't

Farewell to Earth

need his protection on Hevi-Hevi, of course, but they invited him to come anyway, which is cool. I would have really missed him if he weren't with us.

Even Jordan and his father are here. (I think his father just wanted to get away from Earth for a while.) I'm still getting used to being glad to have Jordan with us.

We're at this field because Meenom said we would need a place like this for what is about to happen. There are a ton of reporters here, of course, but they're all held back behind a police line.

Wait—wait! It's starting. The starship has blinked into sight!

Now it's settling to the ground. Meenom told us we needed something like this to take all of us, something bigger than the embassy. But until this moment I didn't understand how big—or how beautiful!

I can't believe how quiet it is. I can feel a slight wind, just because of its size. Three legs just came down from the bottom. Each one is as thick as a good-size tree trunk. Given the size of the ship, they seem like matchsticks. But that's the alien technology for you.

It's landed. It's landed!

Bruce Coville

The door is opening. There's Pleskit and his Fatherly One! They're waving to us. And Linnsy *vec* Bur are standing behind them. Mr. and Mrs. Vanderhof, who are standing behind me, burst into tears — though I can't tell if it is because of happiness at seeing their daughter, or distress over what she has become.

Now there's a ramp coming out. It stretches from the ship to the ground.

The class steps aside so I can be the first to go on board.

"Welcome to your dream, Tim," says my mother as we begin climbing to the ship.

Earth floats in space below us.

It's so beautiful that I can feel tears welling up and this weird lump in my throat. It's harder to say good-bye to it than I would have guessed.

Well, at least this time I know I'll be coming back.

Suddenly the ship starts to move again.

"All right!" cries Chris Mellblom, giving a high five to Michael Wu.

People are clapping and cheering and crying all at once. I look around. Friends. Good friends. Even Jordan.

Farewell to Earth

Rafaella slips her hand into mine.

McNally smiles and nods.

I turn back to the window.

Earth is dwindling as the ship picks up speed. Without warning we shoot forward, and, just like that, the planet becomes a speck, then nothing.

I hear oohs and ahs all around me and turn forward.

Oh my God, the stars, the stars . . .

Everyone is crying, including me. I don't know

whether it's from fear or from joy or just from how astonishing it is to see the unfamiliar universe stretching ahead of us, the future more open than we ever could have imagined.

"I guess you were right, Tim," says Mom.

"What do you mean?"

"You always claimed that humankind has a date with the stars." She shakes her head and squeezes my shoulder. "But who would have believed *we* would be the first to go?"

"The first," I say. "But not the last."

The adventure is just beginning.

CHAPTER 26

[P L E S K I T]
A LETTER HOME

FROM: Pleskit Meenom, aboard the spaceship
Winkle 'N-Tyme
TO: Maktel Geebrit, on the beloved Planet
Hevi-Hevi

Dear Maktel:

Well, there you have it. My last adventure on Earth. It's been a fascinating, frightening year, with more weirdness than I would have dreamed possible when I first came here.

I have made friends and a few enemies.

I have learned a great deal about life.

And now I am coming home.

But not alone.

I'm bringing the entire sixth grade with me!

Tell me, do you think our planet is ready for an invasion of Earthlings?

Well, whatever happens, it's going to be an interesting year, of that much I am certain.

I'll see you soon.

Fremmix Bleeblom!

Your pal,

Pleskit

A GLOSSARY OF ALIEN TERMS

Following are definitions for the alien words and phrases appearing for the first time in *Farewell to Earth*. The number after a definition indicates the chapter where the word first appeared.

For most words, we are only giving the spelling. In actual usage, of course, many Hevi-Hevian words are accompanied by smells and/or body sounds.

Definitions of other extraterrestrial words appearing in this book can be found in the volumes of the Sixth-Grade Alien series where they were first used.

FORZLE: A scornful term derived from the old Hevi-Hevian nursery rhyme "Forzle and His Bank Account," about a man who becomes so obsessed with his money that he neglects all the other aspects of his life, including his health, his inner being, and his childlings. The final verse tells how he was found dead among a stack of papers on which he had been calculating his net worth. (6)

CORRISSMUS: The whispering of the wind through the wampfields just as twilight is falling. Recordings of this sound are often played in nurseries to calm recently hatched Hevi-Hevians. The word is a favorite of poets, songwriters, and romance seekers. (6)

FLOOGROT: One of the seven sweet but unpredictable spices grown on the planet Ploodangi. The spices are known as "unpredictable" because despite the fact that they are universally perceived as being utterly delicious, they have side effects that vary widely from species to species. Recorded reactions include wild jabbering, stony silence, tingling toes, and unexpected philosophical insights. No deaths have been reported. (4)